# The
# SILENT
# WOMAN

## SHADE OF THE REAPER BOOK 4

# KEITH ROMMEL

MILFORD
HOUSE

an imprint of Sunbury Press, Inc.
Mechanicsburg, PA USA

## MILFORD HOUSE

an imprint of Sunbury Press, Inc.
Mechanicsburg, PA USA

NOTE: This is a work of fiction. Names, characters, places and incidents are the product of the author's imagination or are used fictitiously, and any resemblance to actual persons, living or dead, business establishments, events or locales is entirely coincidental.

For information about special discounts for bulk purchases, please contact Sunbury Press Orders Dept. at (855) 338-8359 or orders@sunburypress.com.

To request one of our authors for speaking engagements or book signings, please contact Sunbury Press Publicity Dept. at publicity@sunburypress.com.

FIRST MILFORD HOUSE PRESS EDITION: August 2020

Set in Adobe Garamond | Interior design by Crystal Devine | Cover design by Lawrence Knorr | Edited by Jennifer Cappello.

Publisher's Cataloging-in-Publication Data
Names: Rommel, Keith, author.
Title: The silent woman / Keith Rommel.
Description: First trade paperback edition. | Mechanicsburg, PA : Milford House Press, 2020.
Summary: An incarcerated schizophrenic is tormented by a controlling bunkmate seeking to unearth the demons of her past.
Identifiers: ISBN : 1-978-620064-44-3 (softcover).
Subjects: FICTION / Thrillers / Psychological | FICTION / Psychological.

Product of the United States of America
0 1 1 2 3 5 8 13 21 34 55

*Continue the Enlightenment!*

# FROM THE AUTHOR

*The Cursed Man, Lurking Man, Sinful Man*, and now *The Silent Woman* all share something in common besides the series name and theme.

I have remained mostly quiet about this but feel it is time to let you know that, although these books are works of fiction, they are indeed all based on true events.

As you read this book, I ask you to be kind to others. Our words and actions have lasting repercussions. When you finish this book, I ask that you continue to do just that: be kind. The world could use it. Mine and yours.

Now let's break the silence . . .

# PROLOGUE

## FATE

*Present day.*

"Shit," Margaret Gerner said as she looked at the clock hanging on the wall. She pulled her smartphone out of her back pocket, peeved at the device. Poking at the touchscreen, she swiped through the different pages and found the alarm clock application.

"What's so smart about this thing if it can't go off when it's supposed to?" she said.

She touched the symbol for the clock, and the application opened.

"Damn it," she said. She had set the alarm to remind herself of an appointment she had for work and set it to a.m. instead of p.m. She hated having late assignments because she often lost herself in tasks, and the risk of something like this happening was always a possibility. She closed her eyes and tilted her head back; the disappointment ran deep and settled on her shoulders like a heavy weight, bringing with it stiffness and irritation.

"How can you be careless?"

She didn't have much time if she was going to make it to the facility her boss had assigned her to. Although it was an exciting undertaking, she supposed it wasn't thrilling enough to keep her from being distracted by her daily tasks. Being a freelance writer was easy, but the hours varied so much from day to day, it was no wonder she got mixed up.

She needed to cover this story, and in order to do that, she needed to get there in a hurry. In this situation there could be no "if." It was a must. Her job depended on it.

The instructions were simple and clear. She was to go to the facility and write her report on her experiences. Despite her lateness against deadlines, she had been given full freedom. It came after apologies and a promise to prove her worthiness.

After she was done covering her experiences, the film crew was going to the location to get some shots so people knew exactly what this little-known place looked like. The graphics to go along with her documentary would make the program like the colors that make a rainbow.

"Delay the film crew and suffer the consequences," she had heard her boss say a million times. It was often said in jest to the reporters who were assigned special tasks such as this, but she knew it wasn't a joke. These guys were expensive and on a strict time schedule as well, bouncing from location to location, working against a deadline more grueling than her own to get their footage to the editorial team.

Having witnessed the film crew working, they would descend upon a place and would work quickly to get multiple shots, then move on like an organized mob making a kill and getting out as fast as possible.

She had seen a ton of people with their heads on the chopping block because they dared to interfere with the film crew by being late or not managing their time within the assignment appropriately. If she didn't move her ass, she would find herself on the block like so many before her, and there was no doubt she would see the hatchet coming right for her neck this time.

"I'm going to get there if it kills me," she said and hurried around the house looking for her car keys.

"Oh, come on!"

She looked at the rack with the hooks by the garage, and they weren't there. To the left of the refrigerator was the stack of mail she had taken in when she got home from going grocery shopping earlier in the day. Shuffling through that paperwork in haste she didn't find them there either.

Turning with a sigh she moved to the center of the kitchen and closed her eyes and rubbed her temples.

"C'mon, think."

She lowered her head and went back over her steps, tapping her foot as her mind moved her through the house, retracing every step since she arrived home. Then she remembered and hurried into the bathroom. They were there, beside the sink. She recalled she had to pee really badly when she got home and dropped the mail and ran to the toilet while clenching the keys in her fist. She didn't even remember she was holding them until she went to wipe.

With no time to waste, she grabbed the keys and hurried out the door and into her car. Starting the engine, she put the shifter in drive and slammed on the gas. She had time to make up, and she was determined not to be late. Any touches to her makeup and hair could be done at a red light or even while she was driving. Her brother had taught her how to steer the car with her knees, and she would do that if need be.

"Because there's no freaking way I'm blowing this," she said.

Of course it had to rain. And when it rains it pours. And when it pours, everyone drives really slowly. Margaret had no time for slow. Showing up late to this appointment would not only be embarrassing but career suicide as well. These arrangements were made for her well in advance, and there was just no excuse. Not the rain, traffic, or a CAT 5 hurricane.

"Yeah, explain this one away, you big dummy. You should've paid attention to the time and not relied on your damn phone," she said aloud to herself. "I got along fine in my life before those stupid contraptions came out. Now it seems to complicate everything I do."

The windshield started to fog, and she used her sleeve, wiping it in a circular motion so she could see. Satisfied with a clearing as big as her head, she weaved in and out of traffic. The traffic light turned yellow, and she sped toward it, determined to beat it. But the car in front of her didn't ignore the yellow and halted to a complete and abrupt stop; their brake lights burned red like a scream for her to slow down and realize she was putting herself and, more importantly, others at risk.

The rain was falling heavy now, and the crummy wiper blades blurred what she saw. She slammed the brakes, overreacting. Her vehicle slid on wet leaves, veering to the right shoulder, and the rubber was unable to get any traction to slow down. The car missed a guardrail and the stopped vehicle by a foot or less on either side and went over a curb and off the road with a bang. It continued to slide and tumbled down a steep embankment, banging loudly as it flipped, slinging her body all around until the car settled on its hood somewhere at the bottom of a chasm, smoke billowing into the air like a signal for help.

# 1

# THE MAN

*The past.*

Stacey took her doll and tossed it up in the air. "I've got you," she said and caught it with care. She spun around, dancing with the stuffed toy. It had button eyes, string hair, and a stitched mouth shaped to look like a smile that was more like a devious smirk.

"Hey, little girl, come here," a man at the rickety screen door whispered. Stacey backed away with a gasp and dropped her doll.

The man blended into the shadows of the night, and his features were completely hidden. He wore a white tank top that was easy to see, and Stacey just stared, paralyzed by her fear, feeling the danger this person presented.

"Come on," he said.

She licked her lips and tried to speak but could only manage a dry dull croak. Her feet felt like they were nailed to the floor, and the beat of her heart rammed the inside of her ribcage. She could sense the danger and knew enough to flee, but no matter how hard she tried, she couldn't get her legs to respond.

"I'm hoping you can help me," the man said and pressed his face against the aluminum screening. "I'm just needing to ask you a few questions is all and I'll be on my way."

The light from the living room cast onto his face. One eye looked at her and the other drifted upward, staring at something on the ceiling. He had a bushy mustache, and his lips were parted by a wily grin that showed his bad hygiene.

"Ask your question then," she managed to say, stumbling over her doll as she backed up some more. Her legs were as stiff as wood and her feet as heavy as cinder blocks.

"I don't want to have to talk too loud." He looked over his shoulder and all around. He faced her again. "Come here, what I have to tell you is a secret," he said. This time his words were accompanied with a beckoning finger that might as well have been a knife.

"No," she managed to whisper and shook her head. Her heart started to pound faster now, threatening to break out of its bone cage.

"What do you mean, 'no'? What are you afraid of?" He reached and placed a hand on the door handle, pausing before he did anything else.

Stacey stiffened and everything slowed to a crawl. Her thinking became clouded at the strange phenomenon. What was happening?

"I won't hurt you," the man said. "I just want to talk to you. Don't you understand? Innocent conversation is all I want. I'm lonely and just want someone to talk to."

Just then everything came back to normal as if someone had clapped their hands to bring her to. She knew she was afraid of his being there and what his intentions might be. Being terrified of the person was an understatement, and she didn't want to show it because it might empower him. So she swallowed hard and looked down the hallway, wondering where her sister had disappeared to.

A breeze from the cool night air rushed inside the living room and carried the smell of bad body odor into the house. It reminded her of her stepfather. So did the stains on the man's tank top. Her knees smacked together, and she had a strong urge to urinate right where she stood.

"You couldn't imagine how defeating the loneliness is." He looked over his shoulder again. "Where are your parents?" He craned his neck as he tried to look inside the house. He pulled the door open. "Are you home alone?"

The spring whined and awakened Stacey's fear into a desperate fit to survive.

"Deb!" she shouted over and over again, her screams growing louder with each call until her voice strained. In response, the man let the door go, and it snapped shut with a bang.

Stacey watched the man run off into the night as if he'd never been there at all. Just a thing from her imagination.

"What is it?" Deb said, hurrying into the room. "And what the heck is that I smell?"

Stacey stared at the door and pointed. "There was a man there, trying to get me to come over to him. Something wasn't right about him, and I knew to stay away. When I didn't go over to him he opened the screen door, and it really scared me. I thought he was going to come inside. I wanted to run, but my legs felt so heavy, I couldn't move. All I could do was call out to you. That's when he ran away."

Deb went to the door, and Stacey backed away with her limbs still stiff and heavy. Her eyes stretched wide from fear.

"Don't go over there," she said with tangible concern. "He still might be out there, waiting."

"Shh," Deb said and held up a finger.

She looked around, searching, and her being anywhere near that door only increased Stacey's anxiety.

"Well I don't see anyone." She continued to spy the dark street. "Everything is quiet." She walked over to the heavy inside door and closed it. Locking the handle, she helped her sister over to the couch and picked up her doll along the way, placing it in her lap. "Maybe it's best we don't keep that door open while Mom is at work. No matter how nice it is out-side. Does that sound good?"

Stacey nodded her head. "OK."

"Are you?"

"Yes," she said, and her jaw quivered. "I mean I think so. That man really scared me."

"I know because I can see it in your face, and your body is really stiff. Relax." She took Stacey's arm and studied the tightly clenched fist. "Open your hand."

Stacey's knuckles were white. Deb helped pry her fingers open.

"I'm just glad you had enough sense to call for help and not go over to him," Deb said.

"I said I know better than that," Stacey said with a dry tongue that stuck to the roof of her mouth. The palm of her hand hurt, and she saw her fingernails had left impressions in the skin.

"I know you do, Stacey. You're wise beyond your years, and that is proof that I've taught you well."

Deb smiled and the mood lightened.

"You're not that much older than me."

"No," Deb said with a growing smile. "But four years is enough. It is experience, and it might have saved you."

"He was an ugly man," Stacey said and made a face of displeasure then shivered. "His eyes were weird."

"What do you mean his eyes were weird?"

"One of them was looking at me and the other was looking up or something."

"Sounds creepy. I'm sorry I wasn't there to protect you."

"He was very creepy, and you did protect me. He ran away when you came."

"I suppose. Is there anything else you can remember about him?"

"He smelled like sweat and wore a dirty tank top. It was hard to see but he reminded me of Stepdad. I know this sounds crazy, but for a second, I thought he came back."

Deb sighed. "You know that's not possible. He's gone, and no one will ever question the reasons why. The circumstances surrounding his death were good enough for the police so that means they're good enough for us. They knew he was no good. Nothing about him was. Do you hear me?"

Stacey nodded with a measure of disbelief. Not that he was worth a shit—rather that his death seemed to have this aura of doubt surrounding it. She always worried that would catch up to her. His death haunted her, and she tried so hard to keep it tucked away in some imaginary pocket that could conceal all bad things like that—even dirty secrets. But she found this pocket was swollen and overflowing, becoming hard to keep closed.

"Why did Dad leave us?" Stacey said.

"Because him and Mom didn't get along," she said. "You know that. Mom wanted him out for some reason. These adult things can be complicated, and I'm not going to pretend I fully understand it because I don't. But I'm sure they both had their reasons."

"Do you think she brought Chad home to spite Dad?"

"I know she did, Stacey. They were complete opposites. Dad was refined, and Chad was dirty and rough. He changed everything about the way we lived, about the way Mom dealt with us."

"Why do you think Mom married him then?" Stacey said. "Does she not love us?"

"I don't think it's that at all. I think she did it to spite Dad. I believe you had that right. There were some friends in school I was talking to that had parents go through a divorce, and they said it was ugly and they would do things to hurt each other all the time. It sounds stupid, I know. They're supposed to be adults, but sometimes they don't act it."

"I hate the way Chad made us call him 'Stepdad' after they married."

"There were a lot of things I hated about him, and having to call him Stepdad was the least of them."

"Me too," Stacey said. "I suppose you're right."

"Well we don't have to worry about him anymore, now do we?"

"No we don't," Stacey said and imagined she buttoned that stuffed pocket closed and put it away. She tossed her doll aside.

"I want you to know that you did good," Deb said. "You really need to know that. What happened tonight could have ended really bad if he would've gotten his hands on you."

"I know it." Her eyes grew wide and wet. "I could feel it inside here." She placed her hand over her heart. "That creep was trying to come inside the house—trying to get me."

"I thought I heard the door bang shut just before I made it into the room."

"It did." She paused in thought, the stiffness loosening and turning into a tremble. Her eyes let tears fall. "I don't know why he ran so fast when I called your name."

"It doesn't matter. What matters is you scared him off, and I'm glad he's gone," Deb said and walked over to the tube television and turned it on. The black and white screen flickered to life, and *Looney Tunes* came on. Fuzz distorted the screen, and Deb fiddled with the rabbit ears antenna until the picture cleared. "I don't know what I could have done if he actually came inside."

"That scares me to think about that."

Deb played with the antennae a bit more. "How's that?"

"Good," Stacey said when the picture cleared. She shivered hard. The man's wild eyes were emblazoned in her mind, and she didn't want to close her eyes ever again. The memory of her stepfather was fresh now, too. It was like someone was trying to pry open her conscious mind, get to the secret pocket, spill its contents, and expose her guilt. She worked hard to push the thoughts away and protect what she kept tucked away. "He must not have known we were home alone. That's the only thing that makes sense to me," Stacey said and thought about it some more. "Maybe he thought I said 'Dad' instead of 'Deb'?"

Deb sat next to Stacey. "That sounds like a reasonable explanation to me. And that means that our stepdad might have been good for something after all."

# 2

# CHECK IN

Stacey sat on a cold hard seat. The strange room had stark white walls with no decorations to add anything to the aesthetic. Bright fluorescent lights overhead hurt her eyes.

A woman sat behind a desk at the head of the room and worked feverishly on a stack of paperwork. There was a rhythm to her movement like a beat to a pulse. Stacey meshed her fingers together and placed them in her lap while she continued to watch the woman with unwavering curiosity. It was strange how pale the woman's skin was and the way she blended into the walls. She would have been invisible if it wasn't for her powder blue scrubs.

The temperature of the room was a little too cold for Stacey to find any real comfort in, and the white walls made it feel like a winter wonderland. The light jumpsuit she wore let the chill seep in, and the flip-flops left her feet exposed; her toes were equally as numb as her hands. She shivered.

"Stacey," the woman behind the desk called out without looking up. "Step forward, please."

Stacey forgot about the chilly air that penetrated her strange outfit, and she approached the desk, unsure where she was, how and why she was even there. Something had interfered with her routine, and the day was a blur of decisions that were not her own.

"I need you to sign the bottom next to the X," the woman said and dropped a pen on top of the paper.

Stacey picked up the paper to read it, but the woman behind the desk slapped a hand on the page, slamming it onto the desktop with a thump. She left her hand on top of the page.

"It doesn't leave the surface of my desk, and neither does that pen," the woman said. Her face turned red, and she bared her teeth. "Those are the rules. Besides, you know why you're here. This is the reason why you came in the first place, isn't it?"

Stacey just stared, her confusion deep.

"You're the one that wanted to do this, so why do you look so lost? Besides, is there anything you're going to read that's going to change your having to go into that room?"

Stacey still stared. There were no words to thwart off this woman.

"No, I didn't think so. Just sign the paper, and let's get on with this."

"I just want to see what it says."

The woman sighed. "It says to sign right here." She jabbed her pointer finger on the X. "Now sign so I can get Mr. Dubreuil to escort you to your room."

Stacey didn't dare challenge the woman now that she seemed so agitated. She didn't like confrontation so she signed the paper without reading it, and the woman snatched the pen away and motioned someone over. "I can't leave you with anything to hurt yourself or others. Silence and confined spaces has a way of getting to people and making them do stupid things. Take this, and make sure you hang onto it. That's all you're getting."

She set a small bag on the desktop.

"If someone takes it away from you or you don't ration it right, that's not our problem. Remember that. We don't put up with complainers."

"Who would want to take this from me?"

Before the woman could respond someone from behind Stacey said, "Is she signed in?"

Startled by his sudden appearance, she went to turn around, but a powerful hand clamped onto her upper arm, controlling her, keeping her focus straight.

"No sudden movements, young lady."

The woman cleared her throat. "I'm not saying she wasn't being a little difficult, but yes, she's signed in, and she's all yours. Good riddance."

"You," he said and moved his mouth close to Stacey's ear. "I want you to understand something right now before we even get started. While you're here we are in control. You do as you're told, when you're told, and nothing else. Do you understand what I'm telling you?"

"Yes," she said, but didn't understand why she was being told these things and being treated this way. His firm grip hurt and she tried to peel it away with her other hand.

"Nuh-uh," the man said and moved away from her ear. "Any sudden moves might be taken as a threat and will be met with force. I'll remind you again not to do anything unless instructed to do so. Do you understand what I'm telling you?"

"Yes."

"Good. Now put your hands by your side. If you follow these very simple instructions, you'll do fine here. Anything else may prove to be a difficult and uncomfortable stay for you."

"OK," she said and lowered her hand to her side, cringing at the pain in her arm from his cinching grip.

"Now keep your eyes straight and move along like your ass is on fire," the man said. He gave Stacey a shove from behind, getting her feet moving, releasing his hold.

"But where am I to go?"

"Just as I said, you're going straight ahead and through them doors you see."

That's not what she meant, and she hadn't noticed the doors until now. They blended into the white perfectly. Pushing through them, a long corridor with doors on either side of the hallway spread about every twenty feet apart held her attention. They reminded her of a place she just came from. In fact, wasn't even sure she made it anyplace else at all. Did she go in a circle in her mind, or maybe she was just in a different part of the facility? The people were different. Of that much she was certain.

The doors on either side of the hallway were solid steel with a gap at the bottom. There was a hatch on every door that shut with an outside lock about waist high. The floor was buffed to a high sheen, and her flip-flops squeaked with each step. The chill didn't let up.

"I want you to go three more doors down and stop in front of the door on your right," the uncaring man she knew as Dubreuil said.

Stacey counted the doors, faced the third one, and stopped in front of it, her eyes trained on the dirty smudges left behind by unclean hands and the deep scratches that bore into the paint from years of use.

"Number five," Dubreuil shouted and tapped a nightstick against the wall. The door slid open. "Inside," he said and encouraged Stacey into the room with another heartless shove.

She turned and faced the large man; the dark-colored correctional uniform, black nightstick, and badge were all she could see. He was a mountain of a man and as wide as any she'd ever seen before.

The door slid closed and met the jamb with an echoing bang. Stacey flinched and stared at the cold metal where the paint was worn away, scratched by prying hands that had obviously become desperate to escape this room. She could feel that emotion rising in her chest already and slapped the door.

"Please, open the door," she shouted. "What am I doing here, and who are you people?" She whimpered. "You're all so mean. Why are you acting this way?"

The echo of her own voice bouncing around the small room she now occupied was the only response she got.

# 3

# ENTICED

*The past.*

Crazy Eyes had run about a half a block away from the house with the screaming little girl and was winded. She'd called for her dad and he didn't want to face him. Sticking to the shadows, he paused every now and then to see if he was being followed. He'd made a stupid mistake, and it almost cost him.

Certain he wasn't being followed, he rested his shoulder against a tree and tried to slow his breathing. He felt safe and far enough away from the screaming girl that he wouldn't be caught. The bulky tree trunk he leaned against had a thick overhead canopy that blocked the moonlight above, providing him with a blanket of darkness so deep it would help keep him concealed until he could figure out what his next move was going to be.

A house—one with a patchy lawn and kids' toys left here and there—caught his attention. It was directly across the street from where he was resting, and it made him smile.

"What are the chances?"

To his surprise, he saw a little girl sitting on a couch, alone, playing with something and watching television. She was just like the other little girl he wanted. He rubbed his hands together in delight. This was too good to be true.

He hurried across the street and tried to contain his excitement by slowing his pace. He crept up the walkway and watched her. She was cute, appearing to be around the same age as the girl down the street.

15

He walked around the house, quiet with every step, peering into every window to see who was home, and making sure there was no dog. He failed to do a perimeter search the last time and it almost got him caught.

"Never again," he said, the blood pumping through his veins with excitement. "I've learned my lesson." He was a hunter, and the little girl inside playing was his prey. He wanted her more than anything. She would pay for his screw up from before if he could get his hands on her.

"C'mon, think," he whispered, punching himself in the head repeatedly. "OK, stop."

He worked on calming his breathing. Anyone else who was home seemed to be upstairs. Every room on the upper floor was lit up, and he needed to play this cool.

*But the other girl saw your face.*

"Don't worry about her. I like this one better anyways. She seems more . . ." His thoughts trailed off as he rounded the house and watched her from the front door, far enough away from the light of the house not to be seen. ". . . innocent and gullible, too. I can get her. This one is easy."

He watched her play. Soft cheeks dotted with freckles and stringy, coconut fiber-colored hair draped lazily over her shoulders and blended into the antique white nightgown she wore. It was as if she had dressed up knowing he was going to come for her.

Picking up a jump rope with pink plastic handles off the lawn and approaching the door, he bent over and made sure he didn't stand too close to the screen. "Excuse me," he said.

The little girl flinched and stared at him with widened eyes.

He held out the jump rope, and it dangled from his loosened grasp. "Does this belong to you?"

The little girl curled up on the couch and didn't answer. He could see her shaking and knew he needed to gain her trust immediately.

"My daughter had this, and I asked her where she got it from." He laughed gently. "It took me awhile to get it out of her, but she confessed that it was left out on your front lawn and she took it. If you identify this as being yours, when she's done with her punishment, I'm going to make sure that she comes here and apologizes to you. Who knows, maybe you can even be friends after all this is said and done. Does it belong to you?"

The girl uncoiled and looked at the jump rope. "Yes, that's mine."

"I'm really sorry," he said. "I raised her better than this. Stealing isn't right, and I wanted to make sure you got it back."

The tension left the girl, and she put her toy down and neared the door. "Maybe I shouldn't have left it outside," she said. "Then your daughter wouldn't have been able to take it."

"You're sweet," he said, and held the jump rope out, suggesting she take it. "It doesn't matter that you left it out. She shouldn't take what doesn't belong to her. Like I said, I taught her better than that. Stealing is stealing, and it isn't right. Here, I want to make sure you don't lose it again." He moved it to the right so she could open the door a crack and take it.

The girl looked over her shoulder as if she were looking for someone to give her approval. After a brief pause, she turned her attention back to the man and twisted the door handle with caution. She opened the door and reached for the jump rope.

"Oops," the man said, and it fell at his feet. "I'm so sorry. I can be so clumsy sometimes."

"I got it," she said and pushed the door open and stepped one foot outside, bending to retrieve her toy.

The man moved with the quickness of a snake. He cupped his hand around her mouth, stifling a shout. He yanked her out of the doorway and picked her up. He ran away from the house, his mind set on moving as quickly as possible and heading for a nearby forest area. It wasn't very big, but it had a thick band of trees and a path carved through it that the local school kids living on this side of town used as a shortcut. The foliage off the path was dense enough to use as cover for what he was about to do. Into the night he dragged her. The little girl's strength was no match to his. The jump rope dangled from her hands and had entangled her oddly in the brief struggle.

After a short run, he dropped her on her head, and she didn't move much. She groaned as he forced her to her stomach and pulled her hands behind her back. Crazy Eyes used the moonlight to see as he bound her wrists with the jump rope, making the knot extra tight. Once he was finished he got off her with a firm push.

"Now that I've got you," he said and paced. "What should I do with you? You made me drop you on your head like that because I'm afraid you might scream. At least it'll keep you quiet long enough for me to know what to do with you."

He continued to pace and pant, hovering over the girl, unsure what to do next. He looked down on her with disdain, her groans growing louder.

"You better shut the hell up if you wanna make it out of here alive. I'm not going to warn you again."

But it didn't matter if she quieted down or not. He knew he couldn't let her go. She was much too precious of a prize to do that. This was his first and greatest catch.

# 4

# ROOMMATES

*Present day.*

"No matter how long you stare at dat door it ain't gonna open on its own for you. You know that, don't you?"

The sound of the voice surprised Stacey, and she turned to see a brown-skinned person sitting on the top bunk, feet dangling over the side. The person had short hair and wore an outfit identical to her own. She was unsure if the person was male or female; the tough expression of their prison-hardened gaze was exaggerated by the poor lighting, and it matched the unpleasant tone of voice being projected.

"So many have been where you are right now, and it didn't work for them either. So stare if you want, say abracadabra if you want, but I can assure you nothing is going to happen. Everything you do from here on in is going to be controlled."

Stacey just stood there looking around the small room. The words being spoken to her were hard like the steel sink and toilet bowl against the back wall. There was no privacy and the thin mat on the bottom bunk was an inch thick, maybe less, and she couldn't imagine that it would be very comfortable to sleep on.

"What's your name?" the person asked and hopped off the bunk. They hit the ground with a startling thud. Tall and thick, the person towered over her, eyes simmering with a quiet rage that she feared and didn't understand.

"Stacey," she said and backed up a step and swallowed hard. "My name is Stacey."

"You soft," the person said and looked Stacey up and down and grinned. "Like a marshmallow."

Stacey pressed her back against the cold steel door, her heart racing, her cold hands now sweating. She was unsure how or if she should even respond.

"You have nothing to say?"

Stacey shook her head. She didn't like this person being so close in her personal space, nor did she like the feeling of their anger. It was like heat emanating from a fire. But the worst part was being trapped in this small room with them, unable to get away.

"Yup, I was right, soft just like a marshmallow. Let's get a few things straight. My name is Ms. Mara, and that is what you will call me. I don't go by any nickname, and I like a smart ass even less. This is my room, and I own everything in it. Do you understand me?"

Stacey nodded; her ability to speak was stamped out by the look in Mara's eyes. At least she knew she was dealing with a woman. It was weird though. The hate she had was neither feminine nor masculine—it was just pure and scary.

"You better hope so because I'm only going to say it once," Mara said and turned away with a chuckle. "Being you so soft, I'm going to call you Marshmallow from now on. Creamy white ass as scared as shit. And if you ain't scared yet you is dumb."

Stacey swallowed hard, the fear in her chest like a hard lump. She had been caged with an animal for some reason and wanted to get out. But the walls were cinder block, and the door was thick steel. She whimpered at what she saw and what little she knew.

"The sack you holding, you can hang onto that for a moment," Mara said and turned to face Stacey with a start.

Stacey looked at her own clenched fists. She hadn't even realized she held a small sack. Then she remembered she'd picked it up at the desk where that rude lady was.

"But them shoes," Mara said. "Give them to me now. They belong to me."

Stacey stood still; indecision regarding whether she should comply or stand her ground left her like a statue. The woman at the desk warned her about this, and how she needed to protect her stuff.

Mara slapped the steel door on either side of Stacey's head and moved close. Hovering mere inches from her nose, Mara panted like a wild animal, and her eyes bulged with unwavering fury.

"You deaf or something? I said I want dem shoes. Now take them off before I beat the shit out of you and then take them anyways!"

Stacey kicked off the shoes and felt that the rough cement floor held the chill of the prison. A strong cool breeze blew underneath the door, chilling her feet to the point of painful near numbness.

Mara tried them on, and even though they were ridiculously small for her, she said, "That'll do," and then picked them up and placed them on the top bunk. "These are mine now. You walk around like that from now on, do you understand me?"

The floor was filthy, cold, and coarse. But Stacey didn't have any choice.

"Yes," she said.

"Good. You see? You is learning something already. This is Ms. Mara's place. Now, what did you do to get in here?"

She tried to find the reason but didn't know. "I'm not sure."

"You're not sure?" Mara laughed. "You a crackhead or something that can't remember shit? You fry dem damn brains o' yours?"

"No," Stacey said. "I never did any drugs."

"Oh, so you know you didn't do any drugs, but you can't remember what you did to get in here?" She shook her head. "You talk shit like dat here it'll get you killed. 'Specially if you some sort of pervert or something. Double-talking scaredy-cat."

"I'm no pervert."

"Then what are you?"

"I don't know."

"Well it sounds like you've got marshmallow in that head of yours too. Ain't supposing I've ever read someone wrong before."

"Where am I?"

"Look around you, Marshmallow. Where does it look like you are?"

"Jail?"

Mara chuckled and shook her head. "A door like that caging you up inside here with me, and you think you is in jail?"

Stacey's feet were completely numb, and the pain started to climb into her calves.

"You're in a maximum state penitentiary, Marshmallow. The only way you see the light of day again is in an eight by eight hole with some steel grating over yo' head and guards looking down on you. Damn fucking perverts taunt you the entire time you're out there anyways. I heard of them showing their dicks and telling you what they'd like to do to you. I've heard of them pissing on inmates that they don't like. So be careful if you get out there. It's usually once a week if you is lucky. You do what I tell you, I put in a good word for you, and maybe they'll leave you alone. But you have a past most people despise."

"What do you know about my past?"

"What I know is sickening and disturbing, and I'd rather not talk 'bout that right now 'cause it really pisses me off. Just your being in this room with me pisses me off. I need to adjust before I act on my first instinct."

Stacey swallowed hard, and the lump was still there, growing. "Can you tell me what penitentiary I'm in?"

"What does it matter? Call it Ms. Mara's Penitentiary. You are mine so as long as we are in this room together."

"What do you mean I'm yours?"

"I mean you are mine. Anything you do is because I tell you to do it. I own you like I own dem flip-flops now."

Mara held out her hand. "The sack you holding. Give that to me, and don't make me tell you a second time or I'll beat you to an inch of your life."

Stacey held out the sack with a trembling hand, and Mara snatched it.

"Don't think none of them guards would come to save you either. You could scream at the top 'a yo' lungs bloody murder all you want, and they wouldn't lift a finger to help you. You on your own in here. So do me a favor and stop acting so stupid and straighten up. It ain't helpin' ya."

Mara dumped the contents of the sack on the top bunk. A small amount of toothpaste was in a foil squeeze tube, and a toothbrush made of soft rubber rolled onto the bed. She pulled out a roll of toilet paper and some maxi pads by hand.

"This is all mine now," Mara said. She took possession of the toothbrush. "With the exception of this." She held it out. "This is yours. Go ahead and take it."

Stacey took the toothbrush and noticed it was soft and that the design prevented it from being used as or shaped into a weapon. It couldn't be sharpened, and it bent under a minimal amount of pressure.

"You gonna earn your keep around here, Marshmallow, by doing some chores. Do you think that's fair?"

"Yes."

"Good. Well you can start by cleaning the toilet bowl with that brush of yours, and use the paste as the soap. I want it shining and smelling nice. You get me?"

"You want me to do what?"

"I'll be damned if I didn't tell you to listen. You gonna scrub that bowl clean with yo' toothbrush to earn yo' keep. You got a problem with dat?"

Stacey shook her head. "No."

"'No ma'am' or 'Ms. Mara' woulda been better. If it was any other answer I was going to make you use your pretty hair as the scrubber instead of that brush. Be thankful I ain't doin' dat. Now get to work. And if it ain't done right, I'm gonna make you do it over and over again until it is done to my high standards. So take your time. It's not like you got anywhere to go."

Stacey took the paste, put it on the soft bristles, and started to clean the bowl, swirling the brush in small circles, working meticulously. She tried to remember what she did to get here but was dealing with a big, gaping void in her memory. She signed some piece of paper and then was escorted to the cell. But why did she have to sign in? That was odd, and the woman wouldn't let her read the paper so she would never know.

Mara sat on the bottom bunk and watched Stacey work with a big smile. "You soft, Marshmallow, and I want you to know that I'm gonna break you. I'm going to take pleasure in doing that. That's a promise."

# 5

# SECRETS

*The past.*

"The more I think about it the less I think we should tell anyone about the guy with the crazy eyes showing up at the door tonight," Deb said. Her words prompted Stacey to turn and look at her with wide, questioning eyes.

Stacey thought for a moment, pulling fingers through her hair; so many secrets. She resigned with a shake of her head. "Why not?"

"Because it is the right thing to do."

"Something about him wasn't right, and I think he's going to hurt someone if we don't tell the police. I know it was only for a few seconds, but I did see what he looks like."

Deb took Stacey's hands into her own and squeezed them gently. "You're still shaking."

Stacey nodded. "He was that frightening."

"Listen," Deb said. "We need to think further ahead than what you're thinking. I believe if we were to go to the police and tell them what happened, they're going to question Mom and ask her why she leaves us home alone. I think they would end up taking us away from her. They may even split us up, who knows? I know I don't want that, and I don't think you do either. If we tell Mom about what happened she'll panic and worry every time she goes to work—you know that. Besides, I think if we say something and they put a description of him on the news, he'll come for you because he'll know who it came from and he knows exactly where you live. He might not do it right away, but do you want to spend the rest of your life looking over your shoulder?"

"No."

"Me neither. Maybe he'll take your silence as a peace offering. I mean are you one hundred percent sure you could say what he looked like and what he was wearing?"

Stacey shook her head then shrugged. "I saw his face, but not the rest of him. It's a bit of blur once he tried getting into the house."

"Exactly. If you have any of the details wrong and they can't find him, he's going to know you said something, and if he's as crazy as you say, he's going to want to make you pay. He's gone now. You scared him away. Leave it at that."

The fear of her sister's words rushed into Stacey, prompting her to pull away and stand up. She wanted to go somewhere safe, where none of this happened, but she had nowhere to go. Instead she picked up her button-eyed doll and squeezed it.

Deb stood. "I think we should turn on the light outside and make sure he didn't leave anything behind. If there are footprints in the dirt, we need to sweep them away. We don't want anyone knowing he was here."

"We can't go outside. It's far too dangerous!"

Deb walked to the front door and turned on the outside light. "You stay in here and watch me from the couch. Keep hugging your doll tight. She'll help to keep you calm and safe. I need to make sure there's no evidence of someone having been here other than us."

"No, Deb, don't go out there!" She squeezed her doll, but it provided her with no comfort.

"It's all right," she said. "He's long gone by now. Trust me, you shouted loud enough to scare him off."

Deb exited the house, and Stacey watched her sister looking around the front yard. Her hands trembled at the palpable fear of how her sister had opened the door when something wicked could possibly be lurking around in the darkness. Her foolish move could grant him easy access, and the idea made her squirm. "Come on, hurry up," she said, and her eyes didn't blink as she kept lookout for Deb. She thought if she took her eyes off of her for even a second, that guy would appear behind her, and she'd never see him coming. Stacy was unsure if she would be brave enough to be able to say anything at all. She was absolutely terrified of the man with the crazy eyes.

"Do you see anything?" Stacey said, and her voice cracked.

"No," Deb said and looked down the block either way. "And everything is quiet. Whoever he was, he's long gone and left no trace of his having been here. There are no footprints, and he didn't drop anything in his mad dash to get away."

"Come inside then," Stacey said, and the words came out drenched in fear and coated with a thick layer of desperation. "I don't like you out there. I really don't like it at all, and I'm freaking out. Come in, and don't forget to lock the door behind you."

"Calm down, I'm coming," Deb said and hurried up the steps and into the house. She closed and locked the door. "You see? Everything is fine. I'm fine and you're fine."

"Maybe you're right," Stacey said and loosened her grip on her doll. "I won't say a thing. What you said makes sense. I don't want them taking us away from Mom and splitting us up. I don't think I could make it through a day without you."

Deb smiled. "I know it's for the best or I wouldn't suggest it. I think it's the smartest thing we can do. We just need to make sure we keep our mouths shut." Deb acted like she was pulling a zipper closed across her mouth. "Hopefully we never hear anything again about this guy with the funny eyes."

"Crazy Eyes," Stacey said. "That's what I'd like to name him."

"OK, the man with the crazy eyes. That's his name. I hope we never see him again."

"I remember him smiling at me through the screen. And even though he was smiling, there was anger inside of him. I could feel it from the door all the way over here. That's why I said he reminded me of Stepdad."

Deb sat on the couch next to her sister. She rested her elbows on her knees and clasped her hands together. "I'm sorry you had to see that side of him."

"We had to see that. Both of us."

"Yeah, but I'm your big sister, and I should've done something more to protect you from him. Just like this guy, Crazy Eyes. I don't know . . . maybe there was a way I could have shielded you from Stepdad's temper. I hate how abusive he was and the way he would hit you and Mom."

"And you," Stacey said. " Don't forget about yourself. He would do it to you too when you tried to defend us."

"That day in the kitchen," Deb said and rubbed her hands together. She seemed nervous about the topic. "We haven't spoken too much about it, have we?"

"No."

Deb's head was down; her eyes looked somewhere by her feet.

"But that's because when we were standing at the top of the stairs you told me not to," Stacey said. "You swore me to silence. Don't you remember telling me that?"

"Of course I do," Deb said and looked at Stacey with red eyes. "But we can make an exception just for this moment. That is, if you want to talk about it now while we're alone. Maybe there's something you need to say to get it off your chest. Maybe you've been holding it inside for a long time and it needs to come out. So if there is anything you want to say about that day, anything at all, now is the time."

Stacey became encased in silence. Her eyes moved to the floor, the walls, and her doll, as if it were going to consult with her. But she ultimately returned her gaze to her sister. "I think Stepdad deserved it."

"I know he did."

Stacey's expression was without emotion. "And I don't regret it."

"You shouldn't. What you did was brave, not wrong."

"I can remember that day like it just happened. I could hear him coming up the stairs from the basement. The clunk of his heavy work boots on the stairs as he made his way up and how the door swung open and banged really hard into the wall. I wanted to crawl underneath the table because I knew trouble was coming, but instead I just looked at him and tried to be brave. I was trying to understand why he always had this bitter look on his face. It was like he hated everything and everyone around him, and for no reason. I had been eating dinner and I watched him walk past me. He bumped a chair and rocked the entire table, spilling my drink. I looked at the spill and looked at him."

"I don't know why Mom ever brought him into our lives."

"Me neither."

"And why she never stood up to him and told him to leave," Deb said.

"Because she had no self-esteem. I think that's what you had told me."

"That's because Dad took whatever she had left with him the day he walked out that door."

Stacey thought for a moment and shook her head. "In a way, I don't blame him. Look at the way she treated him and how much better he's done without her."

"But he's forgotten about us so that doesn't make him any better."

"He's still better than Stepdad," Stacey said. "And I believe he'll come back for us."

"I hope you're right."

"Just because he got some money and he hasn't come around yet doesn't mean he's forgotten about us. He's planning. Kind of like what we do together."

"I hope so," Deb said and nodded her agreement. "So after Stepdad spilled your drink, that's when Mom came into the room?"

"Yeah. And Stepdad told me I better clean up my mess, and then he turned on Mom asking her if she was deaf or something. I remember it like it happened yesterday. He started carrying on about how he'd been calling her from the basement, that he wanted another beer, and that she should've brought it down to him."

"And what did Mom do?"

"She told him that she didn't hear him and that he had had enough to drink, that he should go to bed and sleep it off and not to do this in front of the children. His face turned bright red, and his glassy eyes bulged out of his head. I remember him saying, 'Are you kidding me right now? I'm in the middle of something important, and I had to stop because of you. Now I lost my place, and you're telling me to just walk away from it because you think I've had too much to drink?' and then he shoved her down to the floor and started cussing at her."

"And that's when I came into the room," Deb said. "I heard the yelling."

Stacey nodded. "And if I remember correctly, that's when you told him to leave her alone. You were shouting so he turned on you. I watched Mom get to her feet and run at him before he could get to you. And that's when he turned around really fast and punched her." Stacey paused. "He hit her really hard."

"I know it. I can still hear the crack that his fist made against her cheekbone. It was terrible."

"That's when I stood up, but it wasn't me," Stacey said with a laugh and then thought for a moment. "It was like I wasn't really there, but I was, but I wasn't in control. Does that make sense?"

Deb nodded. "It does."

"There was something else controlling me."

"Anger."

"I saw him standing over her, and I couldn't hear what he was saying anymore. I just knew what I needed to do. He was standing in front of the stairs. I didn't plan it that way . . . it's just the way things were. That's when I pushed him and watched him tumble down the stairs. It was horrible the way his body twisted and broke, but I was happy when his body came to rest at the bottom of the stairs because I knew he couldn't hurt us anymore."

"What you did was very brave," Deb said.

"I wake up sometimes from two recurring dreams I have about that night. One is where he gets up after I shove him, and he comes up the stairs after us. He's hurt, but he's so mad that it doesn't make a difference. We're running away from him, and I can feel him on our heels, chasing us with this frightening determination."

"Oh, Stacey . . ."

"And the other is that I'm not strong enough to move him when I shove him. He's as heavy as a boulder. He grabs you and throws you down the stairs. You lie there broken, and I'm screaming your name. Then he turns and grabs me, shakes me, and throws me. I can hear Mom screaming, and I always wake up before I hit the steps."

"You should have told me you were having bad dreams. Why didn't you?"

"I couldn't. You told me we shouldn't talk about it. That we needed to stick to the story that he was drunk, lost his footing, and fell down the stairs. You said we needed to do that until we believed it to be the truth. That is the truth, isn't it?"

"Yes it is. I'm sorry you've had to deal with these bad dreams alone."

"I'm OK."

"We need to go back to not talking about the other truth anymore, OK?"

Stacey nodded, her eyes staring at nothing. "There is no other truth. He tripped and fell because he was a drunk, and he deserved to die."

Someone opened the front screen door, and the familiar screech of the spring stretching made them tense. Stacey reached for Deb and held her tight. The front door handle jiggled hard, and it sounded like a shoulder hit the heavy wooden door.

"Deb! Stacey! The door is locked," their mother said. "Open up."

Deb hurried to the door and undid the locks. She pulled the door open for her mother.

"The hell you locking the door for when it's nice outside and knowing I'm coming home?" She stared at the girls. "You could let some of that cool night air inside. It's stuffy in here."

"Stacey and I went upstairs to play for a little while," Deb said. "When we came back downstairs, we got to watching the TV, and I forgot I locked the door."

"Well you know I ain't got no key. I lost it, and can't afford to tell the landlord I lost it."

"I know, Mom."

"At least not until we get some of that insurance money from your stepfather falling down them stairs and breaking himself in two. Seven grand ain't much, but it'll help get some food in the fridge and some things fixed around here. It seems like the place is falling apart all around us." She winked at Stacey. "Isn't that right?"

"That's right, Mom."

Stacey fell into a silence filled with a mix of emotions. She was happy to have ended the fear and abuse in the home but sad for having taken someone's life regardless of what she said. At least she believed what she felt was sadness. It was hard to know when so much time and effort was used to tuck everything away in a small pocket that was overflowing with bad things.

"You doing OK, baby girl?" her mother said.

Interrupted, Stacey nodded.

Her mother scrutinized her for a moment before she walked into the house and messed Stacey's hair. "I don't know. It seems like something's bothering you."

"I'm OK, Mom. I'm just a little tired."

"Let's shut the TV off and get ready for bed, girls. Today was my third double, and I'm exhausted. Don't mind me if I go take a nice warm bath and get to bed. Lord knows I can use some peace and quiet to unwind. I gotta be at the diner to serve these crazy people breakfast, so you girls are gonna have to get yourselves up and dressed for school. Make sure you're not late. I don't need another note from the school. They're threatening to keep you behind another year if your attendance doesn't improve."

"OK, Mom, I'll make sure we're up and out on time," Deb said.

Their mother walked partway up the stairs and began to unbutton her shirt. "I just wish you both went to the same school so you two could look after one another all the time."

"Next year," Deb said.

"I know," their mother said and smiled. "Both my girls will be in high school then." She started up the steps again, her feet slamming the steps like an axe to a log. "You're both growing up so damn fast, and all I can do is work my days away. I swear I'm missing out on the best days of your life."

They listened to their mother's voice fade as she made her way up the stairs. Deb closed and locked the door, shut the television off, and took Stacey's hand. "Come on, let's get ready for bed. Mom's right—we gotta be up early for school, and we don't wanna be late."

Stacey followed her sister's lead, moving up the stairs, but both their footsteps were gentle on the wooden planks.

"Can I sleep on the bottom of your bed?" Stacey asked. Her worry was as weighty as her mother's retreat. "I'm feeling a little scared."

"Of course," Deb said. "You know you can anytime you want. I told you, I'm here to protect you. Make sure you bring your doll with you so you don't ask me where she is when we get upstairs."

"I already have her," Stacey said.

"Good. Now let's try and get a good night's sleep and put what happened behind us. I think that would be the best thing for us to do."

# 6

# LIVING ARRANGEMENTS

*Present day.*

It sounded like a slow-moving freight train approaching. The acoustics were confusing, and as the rumble grew louder, Stacey stood and looked at the sealed metal door, expecting something to come crashing through.

"I didn't say you could stop cleaning, Marshmallow," Mara said.

Stacey got back down on her hands and knees and pretended to clean the toilet as she concentrated on the sound, trying to identify it, looking at the space underneath the door. Whatever made that sound eventually scraped across the door and stopped, two boots visible in the space she was looking at.

Mara stood and looked into the bowl. "That's real good, Marshmallow," she said and nodded her head in approval. "Don't think something like this doesn't go unnoticed. You'll see dat hard work does pay off. I'll allow you some comforts tonight for dat hard work and your attention to detail."

The slit in the door squealed as it opened outward and the tip of a nightstick slid inside. It just sat there for a moment, the rounded end seeming to point at Stacey. She stood, her back stiff and her knees feeling bruised.

"What are you doing, Marshmallow?"

Stacey didn't answer. She was fixated on the nightstick. Moving a step to the left, the tip of the nightstick followed her. She shivered, and the nightstick moved rapidly, banging side to side, making a ruckus as if to imitate her chill. Stacey scrambled around and bumped into Mara.

"Watch what you're doing," Mara said, clearly annoyed by Stacey's reaction and unfazed by the clanging.

Stacey covered her ears. "What are they doing?"

"Stopping by," Mara said with a shout, and the sound stopped. The stick withdrew, the metal slit tapped shut, and the feet under the door stepped away.

"That was a courtesy visit to remind you that they're watching you. Whenever the guard makes his round at this time of night that means we have about two minutes until the lights go out."

"What are they watching me for?"

"Because you're a prisoner, Marshmallow, and they are the guards. You're a new prisoner that needs to stay in line, 'bide by the rules, and make sure you don't make any waves. It's a warning of sorts."

"What is it they think I can do?"

"They know what you can do because they know what you did, and it was nothing good."

"You keep saying that, but I'm stuck in this room with you, and there's no way out. You've taken everything they've given me away so what is it they think I can do?"

Mara waved a finger in the air. "I haven't taken everything from you, Marshmallow. There is so much more that I can and will take. Besides, you shouldn't be thankless. It makes you sound really bad. I gave you your toothbrush back, didn't I?"

"Yeah you did, to clean the toilet."

Mara shrugged. "You consume yourself with details that are irrelevant. Earning your keep in a place like this is important, and sacrifices have to be made."

"I just want to be left alone."

Mara laughed. "Well that ain't gonna happen. You stuck in a small box with me, and you my only source of entertainment until the time is right to move you out of here."

"Move me out of here?" Her eyes were wide with hope. "When?"

Mara shrugged. "Today, tomorrow, maybe never. It all depends, really."

"On what?"

Mara shrugged and Stacey's eyes slammed shut. Her shoulders slumped forward in disappointment.

"I can't figure you out, Marshmallow. You so damn confused and all over the place. My only reasoning is you must be coming down from a high of some sort."

"I told you I never did drugs."

"Nuh-uh," Mara said and shook a thick finger. "I've had others lie to me before, why would you be the exception?"

"Because what I'm telling you is the truth."

"Sure, whatever you say, Marshmallow. I'll let you have the final say on that because I don't care all that much. That's not what I'm here for, and we've all got our secrets, don't we? Why don't you pick the bed you'd like to sleep in?"

Stacey looked at Mara with a dozen or more questions spinning inside her head, but the look on Mara's face told Stacey the conversation was over, and it would not be continued or wise to try and carry on.

Mara clapped her hands. "Didn't you hear what I said? Lights out in less than two minutes. We're probably down to under a minute now. Where are you going to sleep?"

Stacey hesitated then pointed at the bottom bunk.

Mara shook her head. "That one is mine."

"OK," Stacey said and stepped around the back end of the bunk. She put her foot on the metal rung and grabbed onto a bar above her head and went to pull herself up.

"Uh-uh," Mara said and grabbed Stacey's waist and pulled her down. "That one is mine, too. That's where I keep my supplies."

"You mean the stuff you stole from me?"

Mara seemed to find that funny. "This is my room, and you can look at the things I took as being a part of your rent. Maybe that'll make you feel better about it. If it doesn't, I don't care. I don't ever want to catch you going up there. If I think you're stealing from me, I will do awful things to you, starting with that pretty little face."

Stacey studied Mara's eyes. This person was intense and serious in every threat she made to the point of creating true fear. This was a person who was serving hard time for who knows what and obviously had nothing to lose.

"Well you can't sleep in both beds at the same time," Stacey protested. "So whatever one you're not sleeping in, if you don't mind, I'd like to use the other."

"I mind, Marshmallow. This is my room and my rules. I mind a lot."

"I won't touch your stuff. Not even the stuff that was mine. I get it. It's all yours now."

Mara shook her head. "Anything that's in this room is mine, and you is standing right here in front of me. Get that?"

"Are you saying I'm your property or something?"

Mara smiled.

"I just want to lay down in one of the beds and get some rest. I'm tired, and my back and knees hurt from cleaning that damn toilet."

"Poor baby, I'm tired, too, but you're going to need to listen to me really close. I've been in this room a long time alone. You don't think you can move in here and just take over, do you? What I do is take your requests under advisement. It may take me days or even weeks to settle on an answer. There's no one you can complain to, and it is what it is. This here," Mara swirled her finger around. "Is what you've got now, and unfortunately for you it belongs to me. All of it."

"I'm not trying to take over anything. I just want a good night's sleep."

"You ain't getting what I'm saying. Either that or you're being stubborn and both positions are starting to irk me." Mara lay down, crisscrossing her legs and putting her hands behind her head.

"I had you clean that toilet, Marshmallow, because that's where you are sleeping tonight."

Stacey looked at the stainless steel toilet. It had no seat, and the rim was thin making it seem like it would be impossible to sleep on. "Are you telling me you're expecting me to sleep on that toilet?"

"Bravo, you have ears that work."

"That's impossible!"

"And that is not my problem. You'll be sleeping sitting up tonight. You can lean your head against the wall, but you're not welcome to use either of the beds or the floor."

"You can't be serious."

"I'm as serious as they come," Mara said and closed her eyes. On her eyelids were tattoos of another set of eyes, creating the illusion that she was always watching.

The lights went out and the room went dark. "Feel your way around. I'm sorry there ain't no lid for you to use either, but they don't want anything in here that can be used as a weapon. I'm sure you can understand how two people might get on each others' nerves having to live in such tight quarters and with different opinions on things. The bright side is you have a rim and a clean place to put'cher behind for the night."

Stacey moved to the bowl and sat. If she sat up straight it hurt her aching back and the backs of her legs. If she relaxed, she sank into the bowl— and she was sure if she fell asleep she'd be sitting in water all night. So for the moment, she leaned forward and rested her hands on her knees and contemplated how she was going to get Mara to like her or at least allow her the simplest accommodations. It seemed like an impossible task so she started to cry, mindful to remain silent so as not to draw Mara's ridicule.

# 7

# BURIED SECRET

*The past.*

All day long Stacey thought about that guy with the crazy eyes and how his face pressed up against the screen door. The eyes that looked in different directions held an evil that was unshakable, and the smirk that parted his lips had ill intentions.

She was able to feel that from across the room when he was there and still felt it this moment as if he were still in front of her. That memory and feeling had kept her up most of the night. She had fallen asleep for brief intervals, jerking awake with a pounding heart and shortness of breath. The only thing that gave her comfort was the nearness of her button-eyed doll and the feel of her sister's legs entwined with her own.

That was her reassurance that someone was there to protect her.

The morning had been consumed with chaos. Deb had woken her late, and she had to hurry to get dressed and make it out the door in time to head to school.

School had been a haze; her fear about this guy being on the loose and the idea that she had seen his face was constantly on her mind, unnerving and nagging, distracting her from every lesson of the day. Her sister's warnings were ominous, and now that she was walking home alone, she found herself constantly looking over her shoulder only to see the neighborhood kids splitting off in their own directions to head home for the day. None of them seemed to have the same concern as her. They walked with their heads down, earphones in, eyes wandering aimlessly, lost in a world of their own.

She stepped on the path carved through the dense forest that was about four houses wide and two thick, which shaved off about five minutes from her walk if she was to go all the way to the end of the block and take the long way. The ground was hard, packed tight by all the neighborhood kids who used it as a shortcut, and at times, a hangout. Midway through the path was a clearing with overturned buckets and milk crates used as seats, poorly hidden by thin foliage.

Right when she was passing that cutout she heard it.

*Crack!*

Someone was following her, and they made the mistake of stepping on a stick. She turned around with a start and looked at the path behind her. It was empty. Whoever was following her had taken to cover after they made that noise, and to Stacey, she had no doubt it was the man from last night. He was here to shut her up for good as Deb had warned even though she hadn't said anything. Her heart sped, and with it, her mind raced.

With the instinct to survive, she dashed down the path and heard the footsteps pick up behind her, closing the distance. Around a bend she ducked behind a fat tree and heard the footsteps settle down from a run to a jog and ultimately a walk.

She breathed heavily and covered her mouth to stifle the sound of the wheeze brought on by her panic and haste. But there wasn't anything she could do about the pounding beat her heart made and how her limbs seemed to rattle.

Looking down at the ground, she spotted a mossy rock and carefully picked it up. She clenched the jagged and heavy stone deep in her palm; it was the perfect fit. Stacey listened to the continued approach and knew she needed to time this just right if she was to get out of the forest alive.

One chance.

One swing.

Don't waste it.

And she needed to use all of her might.

The stone dug into her skin as she squeezed it tight. The footsteps were close now, and she saw the tip of a shoe. Jumping out from behind the tree she swung her hand in an overhead wild arc and growled as she did so. She didn't see the face of the man with the crazy eyes because she had closed hers.

One swing.

One chance.

The rock exposed in her grip.

With a heavy thud, the rock struck him, and the force of the blow ripped the rock out of her hand. She opened her eyes, saw it tumble away, and ran to get it. That was her only defense against the crazed man.

When she retrieved the rock and came back out of the foliage she saw one of her classmates lying flat on his back, his eyes stuck open in surprise. A gaping wound in the middle of his face gushed blood. It looked like a portion of the bridge of the nose had been torn away and the upper lip was completely gone. The boy was making a horrible gurgling sound, and his heels dug into the dirt as his legs thrashed and his hands clawed at the earth. A bouquet of weeds were at his side, and in that moment Stacey thought they might have been meant for her.

"I'm so sorry," she muttered, and she could see he was dying from his injuries. She could hear it and hated the sound. His eyes fluttered, filled with the blood that spilled from his wound. The idea to hit him one more time so he couldn't tell anyone that it was her who did this entered her mind, but she couldn't take the sound he was making, and striking him again seemed cruel. This was all so horrible and tragic and she needed to get away.

Stacey held onto the rock and ran as fast as she could. Out of the forest, down the block, and up the front porch she went. She opened the screen door, but the familiar whine of the springs stretching was nothing but background noise to her. Opening the interior door, all she wanted to do was get inside. It was safer there. She slammed the door shut, locked it, and walked over to the couch and sat.

Her hands continued to tremble something awful. The rock in her hand felt like a ten ton something. Her hands had a sticky layer of blood drying on them, and the grip she had on the rock started to cut into her skin, but she didn't care. Her heart pounded so hard it felt like it was going to break out of its cage, and all she could see in her mind's eye was his torn face.

She stared at the door, not knowing what to do. "Deb, where are you?" she said, so alone, her voice pitiable. But the quiet was all that would respond, interrupted by flashes of what she saw. She tried to blink them away, but it was no use; the visions kept coming. She would have had to endure it until Deb got home.

"Please get home soon."

She needed to tell Deb what happened, and then she'd be able to tell her what to do. Maybe she would even be able to help get the mental image out of her mind. She just wished there was room enough in that overstuffed pocket of secrets to tuck this one away.

# 8

# SPECIAL DELIVERY

*Present day.*

"Are you planning on sleeping the entire day?" Mara said, and Stacey's eyes blinked open. Confusion surrounded her, and she moved slowly with pain that consumed every inch of her body. The stiffness combined with the ache was unbearable, and she groaned as she shifted around.

"I guess that bowl couldn't have been that bad if you were able to fall asleep. Most roomies don't fall asleep until at least the second night here. That seems to be when exhaustion takes over. Either that or you're that complacent with what you've done that it doesn't bother you. It must be nice."

Stacey tried to move, but she couldn't feel her legs. The rim of the toilet bowl had cut off the circulation, and she had sunk down into the water; her hind end was sopping wet and cold.

"What time is it?" Stacey said, her expression bearing her pain. She rubbed her heavy eyes. Mara's words held no merit compared to the way she felt.

"By the looks of dese cinder block walls and iron doors, I'd say I don't know. But if I had to reckon a guess I'd say it's around nine. I hear the wheels squeaking on them mail carts. They come once a day and always at the same time. Just like our three squares. Routine is king here, Marshmallow."

"I'm hungry," Stacey said and rubbed her gut. "They didn't feed us last night."

"You came after dinner was served. You missed it, and they don't care, and neither do I, to be truthful."

Stacey would eat a rodent right now if she were able to get her hands on one.

"Go on, Marshmallow, stand yo' ass up. I've been waiting on you long enough. I need to tinkle, and I don't need to be pissing in my pants on a count of you not being able to get your lazy ass up."

Stacey placed her hands on the rim of the bowl and lifted herself up. She went to stand but collapsed to the floor. Her strength was gone, and the numbness was so intense that she couldn't even feel her legs.

"Look toward that metal door, would you? Unless you are the pervert I suspected you of being," Mara said and pulled down her pants.

Stacey turned away and listened to the steady splash of water that was proof Mara really had to go. She refused to acknowledge her accusation.

"Another minute and I might have peed on you," Mara said. "Now that we have a few moments to chat, I need to know what you learned last night."

"That the toilet bowl is as uncomfortable as hell." Stacey massaged her legs. "I barely slept, and my body is killing me." A groan was appropriate. "My back, my knees, and especially my legs. I've been put through hell."

"I know you were having a tough time because you were tossing and moaning all night long. You were talking in your sleep. Just a bunch of gibberish but you kept me up," Mara said; a bite accompanied her statement. "But I'm not worried too much. I'll take a nap later on. I think you'll get used to using that bowl as being your bed for a while."

"You can't expect me—"

"Oh I do," Mara said and laughed. She pulled her pants up. "You telling me what I can't expect. Now that's a joke. Do me a favor and flush that for me, would ya?"

"Now I have to flush the toilet for you?"

"Either that or when yo' ass sinks back down into that hole you can sit in my pee. I'll leave that up to you."

"I don't like this," Stacey said, feeling once again underneath the rule of an abusive parent. She was big—too big to be messing with—and Stacey was in no condition to make a stand. "Why are you doing this to me?"

"I'm teaching you a lesson, Marshmallow. Learning your place here is important. Probably the most important thing you're going to come away with."

The flap in the door whined as it opened, diverting their attention.

"You've got mail, ladies."

Letters spilled onto the floor and Stacey crawled across the cell with her forearms, her legs dragging uselessly behind her. She gathered up the sealed envelopes, noticing one made out to her and the rest to Mara. Her eyes grew wide and she looked at the return address.

"I didn't give you permission to pick these up," Mara said and snatched them out of Stacey's hand. "Did I?"

Mara moved to the bunk and sat. Stacey watched her, ready to cry.

"Oh, don't cry yet, sweetheart. Our relationship is just getting started, and this is the way things are going to be for a while. Remember, anything that comes into this room is mine. You either accept it or lay there and die. What's it going to be?"

Mara flipped through the letters and picked out the one addressed to Stacey.

"You've gotten a letter already," Mara said. She pursed her lips and dipped her head. "Impressive to get that on the beginning of your very first full day here. Wow, you must have someone who really loves you."

"May I have it?" Stacey said with a voice full of hope.

Mara shook her head. "No, Marshmallow, you may not."

"Can you at least hold it up to let me see it?"

Mara turned the envelope all around as if to tease. "As far as I'm concerned this letter is made out to me. Dear Mara . . ."

Stacey lay prone on the floor. Lightheaded from lack of sleep and feeling the slow growing feeling of frustration turning into anger, she wanted to scream but could do nothing but accept what was. It was bitter and pushing her to a place she didn't know existed inside her, and she didn't know how long she could stay there before it became a place of no return.

"What's the matter, Marshmallow? Are you getting upset with me?"

She was silent for a moment, biting back the need to yell and tell the truth. Finally she whispered, "No. I'm fine."

"Well, from where I'm sitting it certainly doesn't look like you're telling me the truth. If you have something to say then maybe you should say it."

"I want to sleep on a bunk tonight."

"No," Mara said and offered a chuckle. "The toilet is yours to borrow, so don't forget to flush it and clean it regularly. What's with this sense of entitlement? Who says you deserve anything better? In fact, you is lucky I'm even giving you the floor right now. You should be thankful I'm not yanking you to your feet and throwing yo' ass into the corner where you belong. Dead legs or not. You don't deserve shit."

# 9

# SISTERLY LOVE

*The past.*

Stacey watched the front door without care, hearing someone fiddling with the locked handle. They jiggled it with fierce determination and knocked on it with force.

*Thump, thump, thump.*

Pause.

*Thump, thump.*

Stacey ignored the knocking. Whoever it was, maybe they would go away. The rock she used to hit her classmate with was still firmly pressed in her hand, and it weighed her down. The blood was dry and flaking off. But the damage she did to that boy's face was fresh on her mind, haunting her like Crazy Eyes did.

She hadn't moved an inch since she ran out of the forest and hurried home and locked herself in the house. It felt like hours had gone by, and it was the most terrifying time of her life. Strangely, she began to withdraw into herself, playing the moment over and over again like a silent movie. The action had begun to slow every time it started to play again, revealing greater details of the incident.

"Are you in there, Stacey?"

It was Deb, but still Stacey didn't answer. She was in too deep, and something held her there. Maybe the long silence she had to endure immersed her into a state of shock. One thing for sure was that silence was another enemy of hers. It allowed her to think and analyze things she should be working hard to forget. Like the things she stuffed into her secret pocket.

Deb banged on the door harder.

*Boom, boom, boom.*

"Stacey, answer me, damn it!"

"Yeah, I can hear you, and I'm here," Stacey said, but the tone of voice she used was barely audible—even to herself. At least the words were able to come out because that meant her mind was emerging, too. Escaping from the place it was bound. It was a terrible place of guilt and self-reflection. It had its own gravitational pull—it was like giant hands that held her in place and wouldn't release her.

"Stacey, are you in there? Answer me!"

But for some reason they let her go.

"Yeah, I said I was here," she said, and this time her voice was much louder. Her mind was rising to the surface, but a cloud of confusion lingered over her like she had just awoken.

"Open the door right now!"

"I can't."

"What do you mean you can't? Are you hurt or something?"

"I don't know."

Then it dawned on her that there was more to her flashbacks. She had spent the past however long fighting off visions of her stepfather tumbling down the stairs, the guy staring at her through the screen door, and the boy's mangled face with the missing nose and top lip and his body thrashing like he was having an epileptic seizure. All of it was intertwined. Connected in a way she couldn't piece together.

What did it all mean?

The boy's face was caved in, and his wheeze was awful. No, it was something much worse than that. And in that time frame nothing else mattered. It was like she was coming face-to-face with all of the bad things she had done, and she was being forced to stay there to relive them over and over again as a form of punishment.

"Stacey, please open the door. You're starting to worry me."

"You don't need to worry, Deb. I'm coming," Stacey said and unlocked the door and returned to the couch. Although last night the couch had been the worst place to be, tonight she felt it was the safest place to be.

Deb opened the door and looked at Stacey with wide, probing eyes. She placed her backpack down and closed the door. Looking at her sister with sustained concern, she approached her slowly. "Why are you shaking like that?"

Stacey didn't answer the question. It was imperative she stay out of that place she just emerged from. Although there was something alluring about it, it was such a lonely place that ensnared her and held her captive. So she just stared at the wall somewhere over Deb's shoulder, trying to stay grounded in the now.

"Is that blood on your hands?" Deb asked.

Stacey looked and nodded. "But it's not mine."

"What do you have in your hand? Show me."

Stacey loosened her grip on the mossy rock coated with blood and small hunks of flesh. She held it out for her sister to see.

"Oh, Stacey," Deb said, took the rock out of her hand, and set it on the coffee table. "Come on, let's get you undressed and into the shower. We've got to get you cleaned up fast just in case."

"I didn't know it was Jake," Stacey said.

Deb paused, pulling back and looking at her sister. "Is that who got hurt, Stacey? Was it Jakey?"

She nodded. "Yes. I'm almost certain it was him."

"What happened?"

"I was using the shortcut in the forest, and I heard someone behind me."

Deb sighed. "You should have stayed on the streets, Stacey. You know this—especially since that guy showed up at our door last night. You know better than that."

"I know, but I didn't want to walk all the way around the block."

Deb stroked her sister's hair. "It's OK. I understand. I don't mean to sound like I'm upset with you because I'm not."

"I wouldn't blame you if you were. I've made a mess of things," Stacey said and pulled away. She rested her shaking hands in her lap. "I hurt him bad. I think I might have killed him."

"I want you to slow down and take a deep breath. Tell me exactly what happened, and while you do, I want you to know that nothing is going to happen to you. It's just me and you here now. This is our space, and no one is going to enter it."

Stacey took deep slow breaths and wiped tears from her watering eyes. "I was really scared," she said. "I don't even know if that's the right word for it." The tremble in her hands moved into her voice. "I thought it was the guy from last night. I heard someone cracking sticks behind me, and when I turned to look, no one was there. I didn't feel right. It was like I had to get out of there in a hurry, and my body started to shake. I felt like I was being followed."

"So you ran?"

Stacey nodded. "I ran as fast as I could."

"Good, Stacey, that's what you were supposed to do. You're supposed to run away from danger."

"I didn't think I could outrun him so I hid behind the biggest tree I could find just off the path. I found a rock at my feet and squeezed it as tight as I could. And when he got next to me, I jumped out, and I hit him in the face with it. I swear I didn't know it was Jake. I closed my eyes and just swung, hoping I'd hit him. I thought it was the man with the crazy eyes."

"I believe you didn't know it was him and thought it was Crazy Eyes," Deb said. "When I was coming home, the police had the shortcut blocked off with yellow tape. I was so worried something had happened to you, but I didn't want to say anything to the police just in case you were home and OK. We always have to think ahead and be smart. No matter how scary the moment might be. And that's what you did today by coming home and locking the door." She hugged her sister and stood. "You came to the safe place. Now come with me." Deb took her sister's hand and picked up the rock. "The first thing we have to do is get rid of this. I'm glad you were smart enough not to drop it after you hit him with it."

"Maybe we should tell them what happened."

Deb turned with a start. Her brows were scrunched and her eyes had narrowed and become furious pinpoints of logic. "No. You can never do that. Do you understand me? Don't you dare think that!"

Stacey whimpered.

Deb grabbed Stacey by the shoulders and shook her sister. "I said do you understand me?"

Stacey nodded.

"I'd rather hear you say it because when I hear it, it makes me believe it."

"Yes, OK, I won't say anything, and I won't think about it."

"Good, that stands as a promise. Now come to the back door with me. You stay inside and watch what I'm going to do so you know once it is buried it is gone for good. You no longer have to think about it."

Deb led Stacey through the house and to the back door. She held the rock up for Stacey to see and ran to the rock garden all the way in the back corner of the yard. She moved rocks around and buried the mossy rock deep and placed the other rocks back on top, making the garden look as natural and undisturbed as possible. She ran back into the house and closed the door.

"No one will ever know it's there. Remember now, that's gone for good. You saw the way I buried that in there?"

Stacey nodded her agreement.

"Listen, Stacey, you've been tormented your entire life by people's bad decisions. Stepdad with his drinking, our real dad leaving us, that stupid guy last night, and with Mom never being around—what do you expect?"

"I don't want to talk about Mom."

"That's fine, but that all affects you, and I can't blame you for being scared and doing what you did. This is survival, and you have to believe that you didn't do anything wrong to Jake because he was following you when he shouldn't have. You shouldn't sneak up on people. It sounds harsh, but that's the way it is. This will work itself out. I promise you that. It always does."

Stacey cried and hugged her sister. "I waited for you, knowing you'd help. You're always there for me. I don't know what I'd do without you."

"Don't you worry about that. I will always be here for you. That's what big sisters are for. But you have to make sure you listen to me. I know how to protect you and will never steer you wrong. You understand that, right?"

Stacey nodded. "Yes of course. I don't ever question that."

"Good. Now let's get you into the shower and cleaned up. Make sure you are thorough and you scrub under your fingernails and any crevices where his blood might have gotten into. We always try and take precautions just in case."

The two walked up the stairs holding hands; the silence between them was the bond of trust that had formed over the years into an iron barrier that was impenetrable.

"Let's get your clothes and bring them into the downstairs bathroom," Deb said. "I noticed the bathroom upstairs is acting up, and maybe we shouldn't use it."

"OK. Whatever you say, Deb."

"I'll hand wash the clothes in the sink while you shower. I'd prefer to do it myself so that I know it's done right. It's important that there is no trace of your encounter with Jake left behind. You need to do the same. OK?"

"Yes."

"Good. Now hurry."

# 10

# SMALL PLACE

*Present day.*

Stacey had tucked herself between the toilet bowl and wall and was crying into two tight fists. She hadn't contemplated the idea of Heaven and Hell much. It never seemed that important to her, and that it was spawned from religion made it this big messy thing to her. It was this convoluted slush pile of ideas that created division and angst instead of uniting people, and in it was something she consciously avoided altogether.

But in this moment, the idea of there being a Hell became very real, and she believed she was now submerged in it. There was no molten lava or any pitchfork-wielding demons. There was just this psychological torture that was far worse than physical harm.

"You lucky you in a room with a woman cause if there were a guy in here you'd prolly be kneeling in his piss," Mara said. "Dem men can't aim their peckers wortha shit."

Stacey watched Mara climb onto the top bunk. Once up top, she organized things and lay on her back. She grabbed the mail and started sorting through it again, holding it high enough so that Stacey could see it.

For reasons unknown to Stacey she was being forced to live with someone who was aggressive—sometimes passive-aggressive—but always impossible to get along with. Mara made it a point to control her every move and attack her on an emotional level that was hard to combat. Stacey felt trapped in the small cage, unable to stand up to the much larger, prison-hardened woman. So all she could do was submit to this fact—and cry some more. In Hell there was only suffering and no escape.

"Dem tears will eventually stop," Mara said and held out the envelope for Stacey to see and shook it.

"Who is that from?" Stacey said sniffing back her tears.

"Who loves you, Marshmallow?"

Stacey knew but didn't want to say her name. That would only encourage questions or get her mocked or something worse. "No one. I can't remember ever being loved."

"So is this a hate letter or something? Did you wrong someone somehow?"

Stacey shrugged and wiped her eyes. "I don't know what it is. Why don't you let me look at it and I'll tell you."

Mara tore the envelope open and pulled out a piece of paper. The handwriting was big and easy to see through the light that penetrated the page. There were dips and curls to the penmanship, making Stacey relax some because even though she glimpsed the front of the envelope, all doubt had been removed and she was certain it was indeed from Deb. She was the only person who ever truly cared for her. In fact, she had to be working hard right now to get Stacey out of this position. She always did that since they were young, and now she just needed to trust her big sister. She needed to hang onto the belief that Deb would march straight into Hell and rescue her as she had so many times before.

"You shouldn't be reading that," Stacey said.

"Well why not?"

"That was addressed to me, and that's my business and not yours. That's why."

"Is that so?"

Mara sat up and held the paper out. "Then stand yo' cryin' ass up and come over here and take it from me if you think you is so tough."

Stacey might have been mad and upset, but she wasn't stupid. She didn't stand a chance against her roommate. So she just remained with her fists clenched, a subtle shake coursing through her body, and a strong desire to control it, but it was too difficult and the tears kept coming.

"You sitting there is prolly the smartest thing you did all day."

"I can't fight you," Stacey said. "You're too big, and I'm not stupid."

"I'm much more than that, and no, you ain't stupid. You cunning like a snake. But you learnin', and that's more than what you'd done in years," Mara said and lay back down. She skimmed the page almost teasingly. "And what you don't understand is that you ain't ready to read what this letter has to say. You think I'm being mean about it, but I'm not."

"How do you know what I'm ready for?"

"Because I've seen your type a million times before, Marshmallow. Remember when I told you that you were soft? I meant that. Remember I told you I was gonna break you?" Mara folded the letter. "I meant that too."

Stacey stared at her, indifferent to her constant threats.

"Don't you look at me like you is hard, Marshmallow. When I tell you that you is soft and that I'm gonna break you, you better believe it. I've done it to people tougher than you. But if you think I'm wrong or screwing around I want you to stand yo' ass up and stick up for yourself."

Stacey remained and so did her tremble and tears.

"Being you ain't gonna stand and say it, and there's obviously something on the end of that tongue of yours, why don't you tell me from there in that corner where you feel all safe and sound."

Stacey remembered the couch while she wiped her eyes. "Why are you being so mean to me?"

"There are two reasons for that, Marshmallow. The first is that you're intruding in my space. I didn't ask for you, you were given to me, and the more I'd come to know about you the more I detest you. And that leads into my second reason. You just ain't a nice person. So that means you deserve nothing other than what you is gettin' here in dis room."

"But you don't know me."

"Oh, I know you better than you know you. All my suspicions and anything I needed to know about you is here." She shook the letter and the paper rattled. "You curl up in the corner like a coward when your evil stinks up this room and spills out into the hallway. Oh poor you, the scared girl that can't remember shit. Your type is like that when you're on the receiving end of things instead of dishing it out."

"And what type is that?"

"The type that is lost within the layers of their own lies. So wrapped up and confused that they wouldn't know the truth if it slapped dem upside da head. So you can be mad, upset, or whatever the heck you are. I'm fine with dat. You may not know it, but I'm doing you a favor—and I've been doing it since you arrived."

"You're not doing me any favors."

"Oh yes I am."

"I don't understand how you can put me through the things you are putting me through and think you are doing me a favor."

"I'm toughening you up, Marshmallow. Thickening up your skin for what's to come."

"What's to come?"

"The way I'm going to break you."

"What is to come, Mara?"

"Ms. Mara . . ." She raised a brow.

"What's to come, Ms. Mara?" Stacey asked.

She smiled. "I've arranged some special things for you. I'm just throwing out a suggestion that maybe you should learn to sleep with one eye open because you may never know what's gonna come crawling out of the darkness. Things really do go bump in the night here. Now do me a favor and shut up. You're giving me a headache. All dat damn crying of yours is really aggravatin'. I'm just givin' you fair warning. You need to toughen up if you're going to make it through this."

# 11

# SERIAL KILLER

*The past.*

Stacey was curled up on the corner of the couch, and her hair had almost completely dried since Deb had her take a shower over an hour ago. It felt good to get the grime off her skin and watch it swirl down the drain. But the bad things she was fighting in her head as she tried to scrub away the blood and dirt were unrelenting. Although it was done by accident, she had killed someone, tore half of his face off and left him for dead. And she knew it was only a matter of time before a police officer came knocking at the door and started questioning her. No matter how many times she rehearsed what she was going to say, she would stumble over her words because the chaos inside her head was screaming to get out. If she allowed anything out of that pocket she kept everything in, they would take her away.

She also had this nagging feeling. It was that she was certain someone had to see her running away from the woodsy shortcut and had noticed the blood that covered her hands. It was crimson red and had to be obvious. So she kept a watchful eye on the door, waiting, knowing they were going to come for her soon.

Cartoons were on the television and the sounds drew her attention to the picture for a moment. The silly antics of the characters interrupted her thoughts; it was a good distraction.

"How are you feeling?" Deb asked, entering the room and sitting on the far side of the couch, eating ice cream. "Did the shower do you any good?"

Stacey shrugged. Her attention was now split three ways. "I guess." She looked at the door again.

"When you say you guess, that's not really answering my question. And why do you keep looking at the door? Are you expecting someone?"

"I think they're going to figure it out and come for me."

"No one is coming for you."

"And I don't think I can tell them what you want me to tell them."

"You have to."

"I can't! I've been practicing it the entire time I was in the shower, but then this voice in my head interrupts and tells me I have to speak the truth."

Deb stared at Stacey with care and spoke with a soft tone. "You better ignore that voice. You hear me? It'll ruin you, and that's all it's trying to do. If you allow it, it's going to take me down with you, and neither one of us want that."

"I don't, but the guilt inside is killing me."

"Let it go, Stacey, and follow my direction. Beat it down, shun it, ignore it, and do whatever you have to do until it shuts up. If they show, they show. You didn't do anything wrong. That's all you need to know."

"I just can't get the sound that rock made when it smacked Jake in the face out of my head. It was a really gross thump, and there was a lot of blood. It was like ten times louder than when Stepdad punched Mom. Jake was writhing on the ground, and I thought about hitting him again." She picked at her fingers. "Did you hear what I said? Instead of helping him, I thought about hitting him again and again so he couldn't identify me."

"Don't think about that," Deb said, licking the spoon clean. "That doesn't matter because it is over, and you won't believe me if I tell you I think you should have hit him again just so you knew he couldn't talk. Maybe you wouldn't be worrying like this if you had. Now I need you to say that you didn't do anything wrong."

"When I hit him, the force tore the rock from my hand. I went and picked it up because I was afraid they might find it," Stacey said.

"That's good. That means you were in control and thinking clearly. It is good you got that rock. Believe that. If they found it, then they would've found you. Now tell me you didn't do anything wrong."

"I can't."

"You can and you will because you have to. Now I want you to say it."

"I didn't do anything wrong," Stacey whispered, tears making her eyes glow.

"Say it again, but louder this time. Make me believe it."

"I didn't do anything wrong!" Stacey shouted with a newfound rage.

"Good," Deb said. "Now I want you to remember that. I need you to calm down. Maybe I should get you some ice cream? You haven't eaten a thing, and that'll make you feel better."

She shook her head. "I don't want any ice cream. My stomach isn't feeling too good."

"That's just nerves, Stacey. That'll go away, I promise. Just like that stupid voice you're telling me about. All you need to do is listen to what I'm telling you and try not to think about it too much. I'm the voice you need to listen to. Can we put this behind us now?"

"I can try."

"That's good," Deb said. "That's an honest answer, and I can accept that."

A news reporter interrupted a commercial segment that had just started. He held a microphone, and a woodsy area behind him was illuminated by artificial light.

"I'm Barlow Schaeffer reporting live from Crag Lane in Botonville. Night is beginning to fall here in this otherwise quiet small town, but that silence has been shattered by something evil lurking about. If you notice behind me there's a dense forest that was zoned for housing, but the land has remained undeveloped because of the weakened economy. Throughout the years, it has become a shortcut that school kids use on the east side of town, and at times, a hangout for the irresponsible to use as a place to party."

"Turn it up," Stacey said, her fingernails going between her teeth. She moved close to the television and knelt, watching without blinking.

Deb hopped up quickly and turned the volume knob to an unreasonably loud level.

"Late this afternoon," Barlow continued, "the body of a young boy was found. He was a victim of an alleged vicious attack. An unnamed source says the scene inside those woods can only be described as being grizzly. Although the name of the victim is not being released, the crime scene here is being treated as a homicide. The police are asking that if anyone saw any suspicious activity around three thirty this afternoon, around the time the children are walking home from school, to report it to your local station. All callers will remain anonymous."

"Someone had to see me," Stacey said and moved next to Deb. "That's the other thing the voice keeps telling me."

"You don't know that," Deb said, pulling Stacey close. "And neither does that silly voice."

"I'm scared."

"Shush." Deb squeezed Stacey reassuringly, and they both stared at the television.

Police officials were canvassing the area, and German shepherds were on scene, sniffing the foliage. The gaping entrance was blackened—even with the giant spotlights making the forest look like it was in the day-time—concealing the chaos and gore within.

"I'm here for you," Deb said. "If anyone comes here questioning you, you tell them you used that shortcut today, but you didn't see anything. You tell them you use that shortcut every day going to and from school. Your scent and the scent of fifty other kids is going to be in that forest."

Stacey swallowed hard, her hands trembled, and her stomach felt like it was in knots. She hoped she could remember to say that.

"In a turn of events, when a citizen called in the sighting of the lifeless body of a schoolchild that was reportedly lying directly on the path that everyone uses to walk on, the police began to canvas the immediate area for clues and found the body of yet another juvenile. This victim is said to be a girl around the same age as the boy and is believed to be the body of a girl reported missing the night before by her parents. Her name is being withheld. It is said the hands of the young girl were tied behind her back with a jump rope, and she was apparently beaten to death. Reports indicate that the body was discarded without the thought of the killer trying to conceal it."

"Did you hear that, Stacey?" Deb said with a big smile.

"What?" Her mouth hung open, Deb's excitement lost on her. "What did it mean?"

"The man you saw last night must've gotten someone else, and that's where he dumped the body."

"Who, Crazy Eyes?"

"Yes, him!"

Stacey thought for a moment. "It was Tammy."

"Tammy?"

"Yeah, the girl down the street that always has all the toys all over her lawn."

"How do you know that, Stacey?"

Stacey shrugged. "It had to be her. She wasn't in school today. She's one of the smart ones in class, and she's never missed a day. Everyone was asking where the brain was."

"Is that what they call her, the brain?"

"Yes."

"Did you know her?"

"Not really. She's quiet like me and keeps to herself."

"At this time," the news reporter said and the cameraman zoomed in on him. "Police are asking all residents to lock their windows and doors and set a strict curfew for their children. If they have to walk home from school, it is requested they walk in pairs or groups and never alone if it can be helped. They are asked to stay on the streets where they are visible at all times until this killer is captured."

The television switched to a gaudy man hunched over a desk. "Do the police have a lead?"

"No, not that's being disclosed at this time. As far as I know, they have no known suspects."

"Can you tell me if they are treating this as a serial killing case?"

The news reporter came back onto the picture. "I was cautioned by authorities not to create panic, but they are looking at the murders as being connected."

"Well that's concerning, and everyone in the community should be diligent in keeping a watchful eye out."

"You see," Deb said to Stacey, squeezing her hand and lowering the TV's volume. "They think the guy with the crazy eyes that tried to get you did that to both of them."

Stacey sobbed.

"It's OK," Deb said. "This is very OK."

"Yeah," Stacey said. "I suppose it is."

"You should be happy. They'll never know you did that."

Stacey sobbed even harder. "I know you told me not to say it, but I killed someone today. I killed Stepdad, too. Is there something wrong with me?"

"No, Stacey, there isn't," Deb said. She shut off the television. "It's the world, not you. And I don't want to sound cold, but better them than you. You acted in self-defense. You had no way of knowing that was Jake, and whatever happened to that girl Tammy is a shame, but if it protects you, then it's a good thing."

"Yeah," Stacey said and revealed a smile. "I kind of get that now, but it's still kind of sad. I think."

# 12

# A VISITOR

*The past.*

Stacey stared through a thick piece of glass with an empty seat on the other side. A phone with a tangled cord hung on the wall off to her right, and she could see the reflection of a massive man dressed in dark clothes standing behind her. It might have been the same guard who first brought her to the cell where Mara lived. Or was he a doctor? She was all out of sorts.

"How did I get here?" Stacey asked, her voice echoing in the small room.

The man didn't answer. His breathing was labored and made the hair on the back of her neck stand. The lights flickered, and her sister suddenly appeared on the opposite side of the glass. She was sitting in the chair that was empty only moments ago, picked up the phone, and motioned for Stacey to do the same.

Stacey hesitated in her confusion but picked up the phone and pressed it against her ear. "Deb?"

"Yeah, Stacey, it's me. I'm here."

"Oh thank God. I knew you'd come."

"How are you holding up?" Deb said. There was a sadness about her that pulled her face downward into a frown and made her eyes look tired.

Stacey had never seen her sister look so glum, and it made her slide forward in her chair. Concern filled her mind and she reached a hand to the glass wishing it were plastic wrap so she could easily push her fingers through.

"Sit back in the chair and don't touch the glass," the guard said. His voice startled Stacey and she moved back.

"I'm not quite sure what I'm doing here and where here actually is," Stacey said, shaken. "Please tell me you came to get me out of this terrible place."

"I'm afraid I can't do that."

"Why not?"

Deb nodded at the man standing behind her sister and whispered into the phone. "Let's not talk about that right now, OK? I don't trust that they're not listening to us. Remember that we always have to think ahead."

Stacey paused. "OK. But can you at least tell me where I am?"

"Look around you, Stacey. You know where you are."

Stacey thought for a moment and couldn't believe it. "Is it true? Am I in prison?"

Deb didn't answer her. That look of sadness said it all. Stacey realized she'd done something wrong that she couldn't remember and they'd caught her.

"But I thought you said you were going to protect me?"

"I tried, but you gave up on me, Stacey. You didn't listen to what I was telling you, and now look where you are. You've created a real mess for yourself."

Stacey had no memory of what she might have done and lowered the phone. She always listened to her sister, so what about that had changed? Something was terribly wrong, and she needed time to think things through. She went to face the guard, to ask him to take her back to her room.

"No, no, no," Deb said, shouting loud enough for Stacey to hear and obey. Stacey picked up the phone again. "Don't you mind him. You pay attention to me. Our time together here is very short, and we need to stay focused. Can you do that for me?"

Stacey nodded. "I think so."

"Good. How are they treating you?"

Stacey felt tears well up in her eyes, and her face lit up from frustration. She wiped her nose, lowered her head, and hid behind the curtain of hair. She breathed into the phone. "My roommate is as mean as hell, and I'm so scared of her. I hate it in here. I'm being tormented."

"Just stay out of her way and do whatever she tells you and you'll be all right."

Stacey shook her head. "I'm trying, but she has me sleeping sitting up on the toilet bowl. First she had me scrub it clean with my toothbrush. She's taken all of my things, and all she does is threaten me." She curled her cold, bare toes. "I'm exhausted and need you to help me get out of here. I don't know how much more of this I can take."

"I'm doing everything I can, Stacey."

Stacey nodded, believing her sister's words. "OK."

"Did you get my letter?"

Stacey nodded. "But she took that from me, too."

"You haven't told them anything, have you?" Deb said.

Stacey shook her head. "No, I haven't said a word to anyone."

"You need to keep it that way for your own good. Silence is all you have now, and I need you to embrace it."

"I'll try but—"

"Time's up," the guard said and tapped Stacey on the shoulder with unnecessary force. "Hang up the phone now. Don't attempt to finish that sentence. Time is up!"

Stacey hung up the phone and watched Deb stand up and pound the glass with the palms of her hands. "Don't you say anything to them, do you hear me? Not a word! I'll get you out of there, but you have to keep quiet!"

The words were muffled, but Stacey heard them. She exited the visiting booth and had a sense not to look at the guard. His breathing continued to be irregular, and his nearness was repulsive and haunting. She couldn't figure why this was exactly, but his body language made her feel much worse than even being around Mara.

"You've got ten minutes," the guard said and moved Stacey into a ten-by-ten space that was surrounded on all sides by brick walls that seemed like skyscrapers. "You can thank your roommate for this. If it were up to me, I'd let you rot inside that room while she broke you down and took away your will. This is giving you a chance to refresh. A chance you don't deserve."

She was obviously in the outside courtyard between the buildings. The sun shone down directly from above, and the heat was exhilarating. The warm cement pulled the chill out of her purpled feet.

Looking skyward, she saw that there was steel grating above her—as if someone could actually climb these walls. This allowed some security guards to walk around and monitor her. They looked down at her, but she closed her eyes, only interested in the sunshine that didn't reach that far down into the hole. But she could feel it.

"Hey," one of the guards said. "Open your eyes and let me see what you look like."

Stacey opened her eyes, remembering what Mara had said about them pissing or spitting on her. She didn't want to seem rude or standoffish. Compliance was the only way she was going to get any amenities so she decided it best to follow their instructions.

"Eh, nothing special," the guard said with a chuckle. "But I see the crazy in there. Don't you?" he said to the other guard.

The other guard laughed. "I didn't need her to open her eyes to know that."

"Yeah, me neither. I just wanted to see if she was worth a memory."

"She ain't worth the air she's breathing if you ask me. Not many women are that come here. It's a shame, really."

Stacey looked away and walked the perimeter of the square pen. The warmth of the ground felt so good she thought about lying down but flexed her toes instead. She could feel them for the first time since she arrived last night. The warmth on her shoulders and neck was like a massage, and the air was crisp and clean. She wished she could have more time out here—even though the guards mocked her.

That she could handle. It had so much less meaning to her than what Mara had to say. Distance aided in that.

Bending and stretching, she worked out the kinks in her muscles from having to scrub the toilet and then sleep on it. Feeling as though she might break, she fought through the pain and embraced the few minutes of freedom she had left.

"Marshmallow," the guard above said to her, and she stopped. "That's what she calls you, isn't it? She said it's because you're soft."

She started to stretch again, knowing she needed to change her strategy and ignore them. Twisting and rubbing the backs of her legs she felt the bruising, deep and sensitive. The rim of that toilet bowl might as well have been the blade of a knife.

Not more than an inch from her face something appeared, and she jumped back, startled. A doll with button eyes, string for hair, and a sewn-in smile dangled from a string that was wrapped around its neck. The peculiar doll gave her a sense of peace, and she reached out a hand to take it. But it was lifted upward, and she watched an officer attempt to bring it to the top.

Stacey managed to grasp the feet and he held the string at the neck and both pulled. Cotton rained down all around her, and soon the decapitated doll tumbled down and landed at her feet.

Saddened by what she saw, she wanted to pick up the scattered pieces and put them back together again. That way she could nurture it and have something to call her own. But the door swung open and the security guard stepped into the doorway.

"Time to go."

"I'd like the doll they threw down at me."

"Leave it. It's better off there than with you."

Stacey knew well enough not to argue or look at the guard. She exited the courtyard, and the chill of the tile prison floor stole her warmth and joy—and with it she could feel the misery of the prison's cold grasp sink deep into her very soul and fracture her will to carry on.

# 13

# BENDING THE RULES

*The past.*

Stacey grabbed the handle on the front door and looked over her shoulder both ways. She was careful that no one had followed her home. On the way, she thought about using the shortcut through the forest to see what the police had left behind, but it was still taped off, and she didn't want to be careless.

An obvious strong police presence would have kept the killer in hiding, but little did they know she was one of them. Accident or not, childhood innocence perceived through a constant quietness, she killed someone. No—she killed multiple times if you count her stepdad.

"Hey, Stacey."

Stacey gasped and turned to see Larry. He was a classmate who lived across the street, and he was standing about five feet behind her, but she hadn't even heard him approach. His face was covered with freckles and his bright red hair made his skin look as white as cotton. He held a ball, threw it up in the air, and caught it. She found it strange that he was even there because she hardly spoke to him. Maybe she had said hello to him five times at best, and nothing more. Truth be told, she wouldn't remember his name if it wasn't for his unique looks.

"I didn't mean to scare you," he said. "I was wondering if you wanted to play ball for a little while." He bounced the ball. "I'm really bored and don't want to sit in the house if I don't have to. My mother suggested I ask if we could play. I've been wanting to ask you for a long time but was afraid you would tell me no. My mom said I would never know unless I asked."

She thought to deny his request at first, knowing Deb would be displeased with any other decision. But she thought it might be a good idea to see what he was up to and what he knew. In all the time they lived across the street from one another, she never even saw what his mother or father looked like. With recent events and her fear of having been seen running from the shortcut, she couldn't just ignore his sudden and abrupt invitation. Maybe he had something on her, and the need to know whether that was true or not would eat at her all night long.

"Sure, I'd love to play," she said.

They went to the sidewalk and bounced the ball back and forth to one another in awkward silence at first. A gentle breeze made everything seem so calm, but on the inside of Stacey a storm was brewing, and she was as nervous as hell.

"It's really scary what happened to Jake and Tammy," Larry said.

He tossed the ball, and Stacey let it bounce once before she reached for it. She thought that was an odd first thing for him to say, but it was better than the quiet.

"I know it is," she said and caught the ball, relieved that the silence was broken. "Did you see anything or anyone?" She couldn't look him in the eyes for fear of the answer. "I know the police are looking for people that might have seen something to come forward. If you saw something, you should do as they ask so they can catch the killer."

"No," Larry said and shook his head. "I didn't see anything, but I wish I did because I'm not afraid of the person that's doing this to my friends."

"You're very brave," she said and tossed the ball back. A sense of relief came over her, and she allowed a playful chuckle to escape. Her throw was off skew, and Larry had to chase it down.

"Sorry."

"It's OK."

"I am," she said.

Larry looked at her. "You are what?"

"Afraid of whoever is doing this to the kids in our neighborhood."

"Oh yeah," Larry said and dribbled the ball. He stood back in the spot he was in before Stacey's poor throw. "But don't worry, Stacey. If you want, I'll watch over you from my window and make sure you're OK. You know, check on you every once in a while."

Larry pointed at his bedroom window, which was on the second floor.

"You would do that for me?"

"Of course," Larry said. The firmness of his words reinforced his bravery. "Right from up there every night where I get the high ground and can see everything."

"That's very nice of you."

Stacey looked at the window, saw the heavy curtains, and couldn't hide the smile that showed her teeth. It was a smile of appreciation and relief because she was confident he hadn't seen anything. Also knowing that she had someone besides Deb to care about her was something she hadn't experienced before. Butterflies were in her chest, and although unfamiliar, the feeling was good. "I would like that very much."

"Is your mom still working a lot?"

Stacey eyed him, unsure if she should answer. "Promise me you won't tell anyone if I answer that? I'm afraid she might get into trouble."

"OK, I promise," Larry said and crossed his heart.

Stacey nodded. "Yeah, she still works a lot, and I hardly see her. With Stepdad gone, she's trying to cover the expenses, and she picks up extra shifts all the time to do so. There are times I don't even see her for a whole day."

"That must be a total bummer."

Stacey shrugged. "I don't feel bad for her because she brought a bad man into our house and kicked out my dad for him."

"Do you miss your real dad being around?"

"More than you'll ever know. But I think he'll be back soon."

Larry smiled. "That's good. I hope you're right."

"Stacey!" she heard, shouted in the distance. She looked to see Deb walking down the street in a hurried pace, starting to jog until she reached her sister.

"Hey, Deb," Stacey said, and Larry remained quiet, watching Stacey with interest.

"Hey, Stacey." She looked at Larry then turned away as if he wasn't even there. "What are you doing outside?" She inserted herself between the two of them. "You know the rules," she whispered. "With everything that's going on I'm surprised to see you break them."

Stacey whispered. "I just thought it would be nice to get out. Besides, Larry is here with me, and the police said to make sure that we're in groups. We're doing what they said."

"You're not to be outside when I'm not home," Deb said through clenched teeth. "That's the rules. Now let's get inside the house."

"But you're home now, and I'd like to play a little more. I'm having fun."

"Maybe tomorrow," Deb said, her voice no longer hushed. "You have homework to do, and I've got to make dinner."

Stacey's shoulders fell forward. "OK. I gotta go, Larry. Would you like to walk to and from school together? The police said we should stay in groups or pairs if we can help it. I'll meet you in the morning right here."

"That would be nice," Larry said. "I can tell you it'll be much better than walking alone. I'll see you in the morning. I'll meet you right here."

"OK, I'll see you then," Stacey said and followed Deb into the house.

Deb secured the door, put her books down, and found Stacey in the kitchen, standing with the refrigerator open.

"Since when do you talk to Firehead Larry?"

Stacey turned away from the fridge and the door slowly closed, tapping shut. "Since he came over and asked me to come out and play catch with him. And that's a stupid nickname. He's really nice."

"You made it up, mocking him from your window whenever you saw him outside."

"Well I was wrong about him, and it's a stupid nickname."

"Why did you go out there with him?"

"I already told you. He showed up just as I got home from school and he had a ball and asked if I wanted to play."

"You don't find that a bit odd?" Deb said and raised a brow. "Is he watching you or something? Does he know something?"

"That's the main reason I agreed to play with him. I wanted to find out what he was up to and what he knew."

"And?"

"Nothing. He didn't know a thing."

"Are you sure of that?"

Stacey nodded. "I'm positive. I asked if he knew anything, and he said he didn't, and he seemed genuine. I believe him. I told him I was scared of the killer, and he said he wasn't. I think he really is, but he was trying to act brave for me. It was cute. He told me he would watch over me from his bedroom window."

"I don't like it," Deb said. "You better be mindful of what you say to him. I was going to tell you to ditch him, but I think it's better you walk to and from school with him for the time being. Keep him close, see what he knows."

"OK."

"Mom is pulling a triple. She came home earlier this afternoon, took a nap, and returned to work. She won't be home until we've already left for school in the morning."

Stacey sighed. "Again?"

"Yes again. She's doing what she can to provide for us. You should be thankful."

"I am, I guess. It's just that I wish we had some time with her. Any time I do see her, she's too exhausted and goes upstairs and takes a bath then goes right to sleep. I'm beginning to forget what she looks like."

"You can't blame her for that. She's trying to hold the family together."

"I know she is," Stacey said and pictured her stepdad tumbling down the flight of stairs. "I don't think it's fair to her especially because I created the situation. I guess I just feel bad."

"You did not create anything, so you better stop saying it!"

"I did too. I did it out of anger!"

"What you did was out of self-defense! Don't you ever say otherwise ever again, I'm not kidding! Do you understand me? You're really making me mad."

Stacey's shoulders slumped forward. She knew Deb was only trying to protect her. "Yes, sure, I get it."

"Good. Now let's start over again."

Stacey nodded. "OK."

"The upstairs bathroom is out of order," Deb said. "I went to use it, and the toilet is clogged real bad. Sewer water is backing up into the sink and tub. It's really nasty so I locked the door from the inside so neither one of us forgets and tries to use it."

"How long is it going to be like that?"

Deb shrugged. "How should I know? I told Mom, and she said it'll be a while before we have enough money to get a plumber out here to fix it, so she asked that I lock it off to make sure we don't forget. So that's what I did."

"I wish Mom didn't have to work two jobs and that we didn't have to eat peanut butter and jelly every night for dinner. It's bad enough I have to eat it at school every day."

Deb looked worried. "Please tell me you're not throwing the sandwiches away, are you?"

"No. I know that's all we've got. I'm just getting sick of them is all."

"I know," Deb said. "I am too, but we should be thankful we have anything at all."

Deb grabbed some plates and the bread and Stacey got the peanut butter and jelly. They met at the table.

"I set up some buckets in the freezer and three ice trays. It's important that we're filling the buckets every chance we get and making new ice. Do you think I can rely on you to do that job?"

"Of course, but why are we doing that?"

"I'm planning a surprise party for Mom, and I want to start preparing," Deb said. "If we make it ourselves it'll be much cheaper."

"OK."

"It's important that you remember because we need lots of ice," Deb said. "As the buckets fill, I'll make bags and see if one of our neighbors would store the ice until the party. We'll get some soda and meat to make some sandwiches. We'll have a really good day with her—you know, make it special. It'll be a nice surprise for her as a thank you for all her hard work. It'll be a mother and daughters' day."

"How do you expect to get the money to do that?"

Deb smiled. "I've been hitting the end of the lunch line at school, asking everyone for their change. I've already raised over ten bucks!"

Stacey smiled. "You're not only smart, but you're thoughtful, too. I'm really excited you told me about this! It gives me something to look forward to."

"Me too."

"And you know I'm good at keeping secrets so I won't say anything," Stacey said.

"You're great at keeping secrets. One of the best, in fact. That's an important trait because it shows you're trustworthy."

Deb began to spread the jelly.

"Sometimes I feel dishonest."

"I told you to stop thinking like that. Negative thoughts are only going to hold you back. You get that, don't you?"

"Yeah."

"So quit it. Zip it, lock it, and put it in your pocket."

Stacey cringed at that. How could she explain the idea that she had this pocket in her head where she kept her secrets, and she felt like it was overflowing?

Deb didn't appear to notice Stacey's stress as she spread the peanut butter.

# 14

# TRADES

*Present day.*

The hatch on the cell door whined as it opened. An aluminum tray with a generous portion of food on it was placed on the small ledge, teetering just so it might fall off or stay on.

"Breakfast is served," an unfamiliar voice said through the hole.

Stacey looked at Mara and didn't move. There was no sense in exerting the energy because Mara would tell her the meal wasn't hers. She barely had any energy this morning, and she was tired of the emotional toll just being with Mara had taken on her. She needed to conserve her energy and continue to hope Deb would get her out before Mara broke her will completely or followed through with one of her many threats.

"Well, what are you waiting for? Go on and get it," Mara said.

Stacey didn't hesitate. She took the food tray and retreated to her seat on the toilet. Eggs, hash browns, and sausages made her stomach growl. The smell was so good it was indescribable. She unwrapped the plastic fork from the napkin and immediately took a sausage and ate it ferociously. Although dry and somewhat tasteless, it was the first meal she had since she arrived.

"You're going to have to pick one," Mara said.

Stacey paused, perplexed by Mara's words, but the pain in her belly encouraged her. She continued to eat, chewing the tough piece of meat. "Pick one of what?"

"Which food you're not going to eat and be willing to give away."

Stacey shook her head and spoke with a mouth full of food. "I don't want to give away any of my food. Why would I do that? I'm starving."

"You're going to have to give something away to use as a bargaining piece. And what I'm about to do is for your benefit, so you're going to have to make the sacrifice."

Stacey took the second piece of sausage and shoved the entire thing in her mouth despite what Mara said.

"You'll get more for the eggs, so I strongly suggest leaving them," Mara said.

Stacey chewed and looked at Mara questioningly. She wanted to defy her request.

A second tray was placed on the ledge, and Mara got up and took her breakfast tray. She ate without using the provided utensil. Her fingers grabbed a big heap of eggs and stuffed them into her mouth.

"So are you going to let them have the eggs or what?" Mara said with her mouth full of yellow.

"Them?"

"Don't start asking questions and confusing yourself with details that you ain't ready to face. One step at a time. Trust me, and let me take the lead, Marshmallow. We need to make a trade."

"For what?"

"For the damn puzzle that's your life. If you want to start putting those pieces together we gotta start doing it right now. What I get in return is going to help you to understand. Each piece is going to cost you something, and as I build you up I will continue to break you down. It's the only way."

Although Stacey didn't want to give away any of her food because the ache in her belly needed to be satisfied, she knew it was best to listen to Mara. Answers were what she needed, and if she didn't willingly give up the eggs Mara would take them from her anyway.

"I'll leave them the eggs."

"That's good," Mara said. "You're listening without arguing. Now hurry up and finish them hash browns before they come back to collect the trays. I have a limited window to get this done."

Stacey ate the hash browns, packing her mouth full of food, and then she handed the tray with the eggs to Mara.

"Yeah," Mara said. "This will do."

Mara placed Stacey's half-eaten tray of food down and went to the top bunk. She removed a plastic bag and slipped the aluminum tray into it. She hopped down, walked to the door, and looked out the flap. "Hey," she said. "Are you ready for the swap?"

"I don't see the sense of it." A dull voice responded after a brief pause. "I'm already here, confined, and don't see a way out."

"But you know you must do it to get out," Mara said. "I shouldn't have to explain that again. You said you understood and that you knew how this was going to work."

"You told me I was going to get something for it. What are you offering?"

"You're going to get a full helping of eggs."

After a moment of silence, the prisoner responded. "Send it over. But I still don't see what good it'll do. It's a lost cause."

"You're only saying that because you're upset about what happened," Mara said. "I'm not saying you don't have the right to be, but I know you understand what we must do here and why."

"Yeah, yeah, send it over. I don't really care that much about it and don't want to talk about it anymore."

Mara placed the tray on the floor and looked out the hatch, moving her gaze from left to right before she slid the tray across the floor with a firm push. It skidded loudly as it zipped across the floor.

"Did you get it?"

"Yeah, I got it."

"OK, send yours over."

"I'll send it over when I'm done eating."

"No, use your other tray. A deal is a deal. Don't think I'm going to stand for you not following through on your end of the bargain."

Moments later a wrapped tray skidded into the room from the gap at the bottom of the door, and Mara grabbed it. She took her trade to the top bunk and unwrapped it.

With a few groans that piqued Stacey's curiosity, she watched Mara but was unable to see exactly what came over from the other room.

"What is it?" Stacey asked.

"Something quite special," Mara said and handed Stacey a small withered bouquet of flowers. "You see?"

"What's this?" Stacey said and reluctantly accepted the flowers. They crumbled in her hands.

"Easy. Handle with care," Mara said. "Be gentle with it. At one time it was meant to be a gathering of flowers, supposed to have been given as a gift. Now they're just dead things."

"I can see that." Stacey suddenly found herself submerged deep in confusion but refused to allow it to consume her. "But why was this sent over and by who?"

"You mean 'by whom.' Either way it doesn't matter right now. Place it on the back of the sink. You will need to use that as your shelf. That is merely the first piece to this puzzle, and there is still so much for us to put together if you are to have any hope of ever figuring this out."

"I don't get it." She looked at the dead bouquet. "Figure what out?"

"Why you're here."

She showed Mara what she held. "Dead flowers are supposed to mean something to me?"

"Not yet, but they will. What these things are that you're getting, who I am, and why I have such distaste for you will all become painfully clear. You'll see."

"I don't understand. Why are you helping me if I'm such a terrible person?"

Mara laughed. "Underneath all this anger is a soft spot. Even for people like you. But don't mistake my acts of kindness as a weakness. That would be a mistake."

# 15

# HE'S BACK

*The past.*

Stacey pulled open the freezer door and grabbed three trays of ice. She cracked them into one of the buckets and refilled the trays with tap water. Returning the trays to the freezer, she thought about how quiet things had been at school since the double murder took place. A part of her expected there to be constant chatter of a killer on the loose, but it seemed the closeness of the crimes had everyone on edge and not wanting to talk about it. It was almost as if, if it was ignored, it would just go away. But something like this couldn't just go away or be ignored.

Right after the school bell had rung, when Stacey had gone to her locker to put away her books and get her jacket for the walk home, Larry showed up.

"I figured if we are going to walk to school together, we might as well walk home together," he had said.

"Oh," Stacey said turning away shyly.

"That is unless you'd prefer to walk home alone. I don't want to be a pest or insistent if you're not comfortable being seen with me."

"I'm not uncomfortable being seen with you and you're not being a pest. I'd love to walk home with you." She was quiet. What she needed to say next didn't come easy. "I'm not used to this attention—especially from a boy."

Larry's face turned as red as his hair.

"I didn't mean that in a bad way. I guess what I'm trying to say is that having you around makes me feel much safer. I know I could use a friend and some good conversation on the way home because no one has said a word to me all day."

"Me neither," Larry said, and she noticed that his freckles were a cute complement to his boyish looks. "I think everyone is freaked out, and the silence about it is really weird."

Stacey nodded her agreement. "Yeah, I was just thinking the same thing. The quicker they catch this guy the quicker we can all go back to being kids in school again."

"Wouldn't that be nice?"

Not much was said during the walk home. The forest shortcut was still cordoned off so they took the long way around the block, and when they arrived at Stacey's house, she turned to Larry with a smile. "Thank you for walking me home and looking after me. You're a gentleman."

"Would you like to walk together again tomorrow morning?"

"Yes, I would like that very much. I would like it every morning and afternoon, if you don't mind."

Stacey entered the house, and Larry turned and walked across the street to his house. She watched him until she saw him enter his house. Closing the front door, she noticed the smile she was wearing still hadn't left her face. It was good to have a friend, someone who cared about her well-being, and was a gentleman in the process. Maybe Deb's suspicion of him was all wrong. He was lonely, and like her, he was looking for a friend. Someone to rely on. He didn't have a big sister to help look after him, and he had to be lonely.

"Stacey, is that you?" Deb called from upstairs.

"Yes, it's me." She walked to the bottom of the stairs and looked up at her sister looking down at her. She looked a mess. "What are you doing home so early?"

"I took the day off from school," Deb said with a tired voice. "I wasn't feeling well this morning. I had a bad stomachache."

"Oh, OK. How are you feeling now?"

"A little better, but it still hurts. I slept most of the day, and now I have a headache from too much sleep."

"Well I hope you feel better."

"Thank you."

"Larry walked me home from school."

"That's good, Stacey, but remember what I said. Don't be getting too chummy with that boy. I don't want him causing us any trouble."

"He's just a friend," she said, but not loud enough for Deb to hear. "I already cracked the ice cubes and refilled the trays so I'll just go into my room so you can rest."

Without another word, Deb turned away, and Stacey could hear her close her door. It was rare for Deb to be so distant, and Stacey felt concern rising in her chest. She hurried up the stairs and moved her mouth close to Deb's door.

"Are you sure you're OK?"

"Don't worry yourself. I'm doing much better," Deb said. Her voice was muffled by the door. "Can you try to remember to go downstairs in a few more hours and crack some more of that ice? I'm afraid at this rate we're not going to have enough."

"No problem," Stacey said and went into her room. She closed her door, got out of her school clothes, and lay down in bed. She put her arms behind her head and let her body relax.

It was strange how much her guilt over Jake's death had receded. Larry's friendship and the stupid task of making ice had taken place of that. It was like it busied her mind and gave her something to look forward to instead of dwelling on all the bad things that had happened.

She closed her eyes and thought about Larry and hoped nothing bad would happen to him. He was the first person she actually liked, and she could tell he had a genuine caring nature. She would do her part to look after him, too, because whether Deb liked it or not, they were friends.

Her eyelids felt as heavy as stones, and soon she fell asleep.

Later, when Stacey gently opened her eyes, she rolled to her side and looked at the window. Darkness had placed a blanket over the daylight; she must have slept for a few solid hours.

Stretching and yawning, her belly growled, but she paid it no mind because she wasn't in the mood for another peanut butter and jelly sandwich. The thought of it made her sick, and she would rather go hungry the rest of the night.

Getting out of bed, she dressed in her night clothes and moved to her window. She pulled the shade aside and scoped out the neighborhood. Settling her focus on Larry's house, she stared at his bedroom window. The heavy shade was drawn but was soon pulled aside, and Larry appeared.

She smiled, knowing he kept his promise to keep watch over her, and she waved. He waved back, and she felt the butterflies in the pit of her stomach again. Not knowing exactly what that meant, she rested her head on the chilly pane of glass and pressed her hands against the window.

Looking around his house, she noticed movement on the outside toward the back end of the driveway where the garage was. In the darkness she was only able to make out a white t-shirt and what she was sure was a man. Dread filled her as the person walked around the rear of the house in a hurry. She lost sight of him and slapped the window and pointed. Shouting at Larry, she tried to get him to understand what she was seeing.

"There's someone going around the back of your house!"

He smiled and waved at her. When he closed his curtain panic filled Stacey, and she ran out of her room and pounded on her sister's door.

"Deb, get up! I just saw the guy with the crazy eyes across the street at Larry's house! I saw him run into their backyard. We need to let his family know!"

Stacey didn't wait for an answer from Deb. There was no time. She skipped the steps two at a time, flung open the door, and ran across the street barefoot and in her pajamas. When she reached the house she banged on the front door frantically. "Please open up! I think you guys are in terrible danger!"

# 16

# PIECES TO A STORY

*Present day.*

"Get me them flip-flops," Mara said and placed the lunch tray on the bottom bunk.

Stacey hurried over, reached onto the top bunk, and gladly handed Mara the flip-flops. She was all too excited to have been asked to be a part of what Mara was about to do.

"This will get us something else that's a part of the puzzle. You know what that means don't you?"

Stacey nodded. "Answers as to why I'm here and what the purpose is behind all of this."

"That's right," Mara said almost proudly.

Mara secured the flip-flops on the tray and reused the wrap to hold them in place.

"You'll see, Marshmallow. But there is a price you're going to have to pay for my hard work. I want you to remember to never reach onto that bunk unless I tell you to. You remember that rule."

Stacey nodded, and Mara went to the heavy steel door. She pushed the tray with tremendous force, and like before it skidded across the cement floor.

"What price do I have to pay?" Stacey said and regretted having asked the question.

Mara looked at Stacey. "Learning humility. You need to know and understand it for what you've done. If you want to come full circle, you're going to have to learn acceptance as well."

82

"You had me scrub a toilet bowl with my own toothbrush and had me sleep on a toilet bowl. You've taken all of my things away from me and won't even show me my mail. I was allowed outside to be teased with the idea of getting some alone time and sunshine only to be ridiculed and taunted with a doll that security guards beheaded and threw at my feet. Don't you think I've been shamed enough? I know this is your place and your rules. But when does all of this become enough for you?"

Mara sighed. "I already told you. When I see you broken I'll be glad." She turned her attention to the gap at the bottom of the door. "Did you get it?"

"Yeah, I got it," said the same voice from the first time Mara slid the tray across.

"Good, now send it over to the cell next to me."

The tray slid, scraping across the ground as it moved to the next cell.

Mara turned and sat with her back against the door. She looked at Stacey long and hard, making her uncomfortable.

"I'll tell you what. Instead of me demanding something from you, why don't we have some fun to pass the time while your next hint is making its way back to the room. Get down on the floor and do push-ups. I want you to do twenty-five, and if you quit before you reach that number you're going to have to start over again."

"I can't do twenty-five push-ups. I have no strength. I've barely eaten and hardly had any sleep. My muscles are cramped, and I feel bruised from head to toe."

"You'll find the strength somewhere deep inside if you want what's coming back to this room and to learn what that letter is about. If you don't give it a valiant effort I'm gonna rip that letter of yours into a billion pieces, and I'll have the pleasure of watching you try to put it back together. Perhaps that might be good for you to do if you don't want to do the push-ups?"

"Please no," Stacey said. The contents of that letter were important to her. She believed it would give her sustenance.

"It would keep you busy enough to give me some peace."

"I'll do the push-ups and keep quiet."

Mara watched Stacey get down on the floor, spread her arms about shoulder width apart, and extend her legs behind her.

"I'm counting," Mara said. "You have to go all the way down or it doesn't count. I'm gonna be stingy, so you better do each one right the first time."

Stacey took a deep breath and pumped out five push-ups before she started to slow, Mara counting along. Her arms shook, and her face turned bright red.

"Twenty more to go, Marshmallow."

Mara leaned over and shouted underneath the door. "Send that tray back with what I'm owed for them flip-flops, would ya?"

Just then, the tray could be heard sliding across the floor to the cell across from Mara and Stacey's. Mara moved out of the way, and the tray slid into the room.

Stacey lifted her hind end high in the air, trying to rest before she pumped out her next batch of push-ups.

"Those knees go down, you start over. If you quit—which I think you will—you'll lose something."

Stacey grunted as she pushed out seven more, each one a struggle. Her arms shook something terrible, and it seemed Mara had set a number she knew was impossible for Stacey to reach.

"You ain't gonna be able to do it, Marshmallow. I see it. You're ready to quit because you is soft. I told you that when I first met you because I knew it to be true."

"No I'm not," Stacey said. Her arms and legs continued to shake from the strain.

Stacey pushed out three more with a newfound determination and went down to do a fourth, but her arms got stuck in a bent position, her belly mere inches from the floor.

Mara picked up the tray, unwrapped what was returned, and held onto it. Then Stacey flopped to the floor, exhausted.

"You see, Marshmallow, you is soft just like I said when I first met you. I told you I know you. I'm never wrong about someone when I meet them."

Stacey began to weep, and Mara knelt over her. "Don't take it so hard. You've earned at least what came over on that tray, but you've lost the privilege of looking at that letter. I think that's the best punishment right now for your failure because I know you want that really bad."

Mara dropped a pink plastic cylindrical object in front of Stacey's face. It clattered on the floor and settled a few inches away from her nose. Frayed rope was embedded in the plastic, but Stacey's arms were too heavy to reach for the item. She stared at it, its significance lost on her.

"Don't think I'm going to let you lay on my floor forever either," Mara said. "Gather yourself and pick that up and put it on the back of the sink with the other trinket you've collected so far."

"What are these things you're giving me?"

"Your story," Mara said. "Now don't ask me another question when I've already answered it. No matter what you think, I can't say I like you very much, and I want you to know I'm only tolerating you because I have to. It's the way it is for right now. But there will come a time when I won't have to accept you, and I look forward to that moment."

"I don't expect you to like me," Stacey panted. "Why would you when you've made no attempt to get to know me but instead have done every-thing to expose my weaknesses?" She lay there sweating, trying to catch her breath, enjoying the cool breeze blowing beneath the door, cooling her brow, finding herself on the brink of telling Mara she quit, that she couldn't do this anymore. But maybe as more hints came through she would re-member more.

Buried deep inside she found something that gave her hope. Maybe if she were to hang on just a little longer, this all might make some sense. Whatever this thing she found was, it bulged from holding lots of things. To Stacey, it looked like a pocket.

# 17

# RECKLESS

*The past.*

Stacey pounded the door with a tight fist.

*Thunk. Thunk. Thunk.*

"Please open the door!" she shouted, and the porch light flicked on. The door opened slowly, and a middle-aged woman as white as a sheet looked back at her. Her powder blue robe was tied off at the waist and looked soft and comfortable. She looked back at Stacey with concern.

"Stacey, what is it?" she asked and opened the door all the way. "What's wrong?"

The woman stepped outside and looked down the dark street both ways. "Is everything OK?"

Stacey looked too and noticed she had left her front door open and that Deb still hadn't come outside. Maybe she didn't shout loudly enough to wake her. Or maybe she was feeling sick again and throwing up and needed her help.

"Stacey, are you OK?"

"No I'm not," she said and looked at the pale woman. "I saw a man lurking around, and I think it might have been the killer!"

Larry's mother extended a hand. "Come inside where you'll be safe!"

"No," Stacey said and shook her head. "Larry told me he was going to watch over me because of the bad man that's been in the neighborhood. He told me he would be watching me from his bedroom window. I was just waving hello to him, and I saw someone on the side of your house. He was wearing a white tank top, and when I saw him, he hurried around the back side of your house. I'm afraid that might be the killer and I needed to warn you."

"Oh," Larry's mother said and stood upright. She shouted over her shoulder, "Honey, can you come here for a moment?"

Moments later a really tall man with salt and pepper hair came to the door. He was wearing a white tank top.

"Honey, were you on the side of the house before?"

"I was just a few minutes ago," he said. "I just got in from taking the garbage out to the trash cans. Is everything all right?"

Larry's mother laughed. "Yes, everything is fine. It seems our son and Stacey from across the street have formed a neighborhood watch. I think she might have mistaken you for the killer."

"Is her mother home, or is she there by herself again?" the father said.

"Ray," Larry's mother said, her tone sharp. "Keep your comments to yourself. What she just did was really sweet, and I'm glad the children are forming this friendship. It's good they have each other."

"Well I don't like him being around her. I told you that. There's something off about that girl."

"Raymond!"

"I'm sorry to bother you," Deb said, and Stacey whirled around, surprised at her sister's sudden appearance. She took Stacey by the arm and dragged her across the street and into the house. She slammed the door and locked it.

"What were you thinking?" Deb said, and she started to pace. "Why are you becoming so reckless?"

Stacey was confused. Why was Deb being like this? "I saw someone at the side of their house, and I thought it was that guy with the crazy eyes. I couldn't just stand by and do nothing. I wanted to warn them. How is that reckless?"

"It's reckless because you're not thinking things through before you act out. Did you hear what his father said about you? They aren't your problem, and you know we have to keep to ourselves. We don't want the police to come and take us away from Mom or even begin to suspect you in Jake's death. I've said it a million times that we have to be quiet, exceptionally careful, and keep to ourselves. Instead you run across the street barefoot and in your nightgown swearing you saw the killer to total strangers who apparently don't like us. Now you're going to have his parents constantly looking this way, questioning whether or not what the father suspects is true or not."

Stacey fell silent. Deb was right. What she just did was reckless, and it could draw unnecessary attention to them. Why couldn't she see things the way Deb did before she reacted?

"I'm sorry," Stacey said. "When I saw someone on the side of the house, I freaked out. That's all it was. I freaked out."

"I get why you might have done it, but I need you to stop and think. Doing stupid shit is going to get you caught," Deb said and hugged her sister. "I'm sorry, I didn't mean to cuss at you. I'm glad that boy is nice to you, and I can appreciate the idea that you want a friend, but sometimes you're just better off keeping to yourself. It might be tough and lonely, but at least it's safe. Maybe this will be the lesson you needed so you know that what I'm saying is the truth."

Stacey wanted to protest that she and Larry were friends and would remain that way but decided against it. Deb would give her a million reasons why she was right, and then Stacey wouldn't be able to defend herself. Deb was much too witty and strong-willed in her belief, and Stacey couldn't combat that.

"I think the craziest thing you did was leave the front door wide open," Deb said. "I mean what if Crazy Eyes was in the neighborhood and slipped into the house while you were occupied with them?"

At those words, Stacey needed to sit. That scenario never came to mind, and it hit her like a stiff punch to the gut. There was a sudden lingering sense of dread. Maybe what Deb just said really happened and the man with the crazy eyes found a closet to hide in. He would wait until they fell asleep and would attack them when they were most vulnerable.

"We need to search the house and make sure he's not in here," Stacey said and grabbed her doll with the button eyes. No matter Deb's response, she needed to make sure they did this. She was going to take her stand on it, too.

"He's not in here. I was just saying that as an example to scare you into thinking straight," Deb said with certainty. "I was out the door just about a minute after you were, and I closed the door on my way out. There's no way he got inside. I would have seen him or heard him."

Stacey remembered looking down the street with Larry's mother and noticing she'd left the front door open. Deb's timing was off. There was at least a few-minute window of opportunity there, and that was enough for her to take the stand.

"We should check," Stacey said and stood. "I messed up, and I just want to make sure. Please, it'll make me feel better."

Deb took her hand. "That's fine. If it makes you feel better then that's what we'll do. We will stick together and go room by room to be sure we are safe."

"What about weapons?" Stacey said. "Shouldn't we each have one, you know, just in case?"

"Yes, I think that's a good idea," Deb said. "Let's go to the kitchen and we will both choose a weapon."

"I want the biggest knife," Stacey said.

"You can have whatever you want. I just want you to be careful with it. There's no way we can explain away an accident caused by nerves. Mom would have a heart attack, and that would ruin our chance to surprise her with that picnic."

"I'll be very careful."

"Thank you. Now I want you to know I'm going to be coming home late from school tomorrow. I have a project that has to be done, and I need to use the library. Please make sure you don't do this again. I need to know I can trust you."

"You can. I won't leave the house. I promise," Stacey said.

"OK, come on, and let's get this over with. If he's in the house, he's gonna regret messing with us."

# 18

# EPIALES

*Present day.*

Stacey twirled in her hand the pink thing that Mara had dropped in front of her. She inspected it closely so as not to miss the slightest detail. Whatever it was, it was smooth all around but had strands of braided cotton coming out of a hole at one of the ends.

"What are these things you have coming into this room?" Stacey said clearly annoyed. "Why would you trade my belongings and food away for this junk?" She tossed the plastic thing and it clattered across the floor.

Mara sat up, looked at the gift she'd given Stacey, and then swung her feet off the bed and pressed them on the floor. Her eyes grew wide. "Did you just toss that aside like it was a piece of trash?"

Stacey stood from the toilet bowl unable to hide her frustration. Tired and irritated, her rational side severely lacking, she stepped toward Mara. "You've made me clean your damn toilet with my toothbrush, had me sleep on the toilet, had me flush your piss, and made me do push-ups to humiliate me. You've hovered over me like an animal and have threatened me every time you opened your mouth. So who here has been treated like a piece of trash? Me or that stupid plastic thing? Do you think I care about this meaningless crap you're giving me?" She ran stiff fingers through her hair. "I don't care what you think you can do to me or what you want to do to me because you decide to trade my meal away for some useless piece of crap that makes no sense to me. I've become too tired, and I'm running out of patience. If I'm going to be honest with you, I'm sick of playing your damn games."

Mara stood and pointed at the object on the floor. "Watchyer mouth and pick up that thing you just dropped and put it on the sink. It's part of a collection. What you are given in return for these trades deserves your respect."

Stacey crossed her arms. "No. I'm not going to do it."

Mara's eyes glowed with tangible anger, and Stacey defiantly kicked the plastic thing under the door and into the hallway. She heard it rattle off into the distance.

"Oh, Marshmallow, why did you have to go and do a thing like that? Now you've done it."

Just then the familiar scraping sound of the nightstick on the wall could be heard approaching. It stopped at the door, and the hatch opened slowly. The nightstick came through and pointed at Stacey. It banged side to side like a sounding alarm and then stopped.

"You! Come here," the voice out in the hallway said. It was deep and gravelly, shredding Stacey's courage into a thing of obedience and fear. She came forward, watching the nightstick and noting it was the blackest thing she'd ever seen. She stopped at the door.

"Put your ear to the hole so you can hear everything I've got to say to you."

Stacey knelt, looking at Mara for direction, but she just turned away and sat on the bottom bunk, shaking her head. Stacey moved her ear close, afraid to do so but more afraid of what might happen if she didn't obey.

"You should be obedient and thankful," the voice said. "You deserve so much worse than simple irritation and torment from a roommate, and you don't even know it."

Stacey looked out of the corner of her eye, and through the hatch she could see inside of his mouth. A maw that had cracked lips and teeth that were sharpened to fine points made her gasp, and the foul odor of his breath made her gag. She was paralyzed and couldn't retreat or even muster a scream in her terror.

"Do you know why?" the thing outside the door said.

She shook her head having forgotten the question in her fright. Long spindly fingers with chipped nails slunk into the hatch and wrapped her head slowly, squeezing like a snake and pulling her against the door. The pain in her face was unspeakable as the fingers clamped around her head. Placing both hands against the metal door, she tried to pull away, but she was being drawn in slowly and painfully, being pulled into and through the hatch. It was an impossible fit, but her body collapsed in on itself and filled out once she was on the other side of the door. All the pain was gone in an instant and what replaced it was horrible.

"Pick it up," the callous voice said after his fingers released her like snakes slithering away.

Stacey could barely see the plastic thing at his feet. The darkness she was suddenly encased in was nearly pitch black, but the monster was even darker; it was a stain on the ebon area.

She grabbed the pink plastic thing and held it out for him to see and take if he wanted.

"I know what it is, know of its significance, but you don't," he said. "You discard it as if it has no meaning, and that is an insult to who bore it. And their burden was sickening, forced and inescapable, complete with pain, fear, and regret."

Stacey wanted to say something but didn't. She was too afraid to speak to the thing as it came into focus from the light that shined beneath the door. She perceived it to be a demon. It vibrated with anger, distaste, angst, and so many other negative things that it repelled her, but she couldn't get away and didn't dare attempt it. Long thin arms led into large clawed hands with fingers that hung only inches above the floor. Her jaw dangled open at the sight of it, and she tried to take a step away but fell down instead.

"You look at me as if I were the monster," he said. "But it is I who looks upon you as the monster. You're a monstrosity in pretty skin stretched tight, with long hair and a fake smile. You hide secrets inside a pocket and think I can't see them. But I can."

He had no ears and no hair and a nose that was two deep caverns in an otherwise flattened face. His eyes were wide and red and lidless.

"Stand and face me or I'll force you to."

Stacey was slow to stand, swallowing hard as she looked upon the nightmarish thing, gathering courage in a place of incomprehensible repression and despair, wishing she were back in the room with Mara.

"To discard the things you are being given is to discount the suffering I had to inflict."

"Are you saying I have a connection to you?" Stacey blinked. "What do these things have to do with you?"

A hearty diabolical chuckle echoed around and made the hair on the back of her neck stand.

"A connection, of course. I am spawned from bad thoughts and help to create nightmares. What I have done is a direct result of your decisions and thoughts."

Stacey shook her head in denial. These accusations were untrue and she tried to will herself awake. This had to be a nightmare. She couldn't see herself in third person the way she normally did, but she knew this was a bad dream. But no matter how hard she tried, she remained in the black, staring at what she now knew indeed was a nightmare. And it was the worst one she ever had.

"I am Epiales, and I have done things because you've called upon me. You've called upon me and had me act out on your behalf."

"I've done no such a thing."

"Indeed you have as have so many before you. You'll not disrespect my work but watch in awe of the things we've done together. I am the embodiment of fear and often come in times of sleep and trauma."

Out from behind Epiales, Crazy Eyes stepped and Stacey shrank once again, curling into a ball as she crouched, more afraid of him than the nightmare entity and Mara combined.

"If you would have come to me when I called to you from your door, that other child wouldn't have had to suffer like she did," Crazy Eyes said, and she could feel him draw close, his words and presence pressing down on her. He was so close that she could smell him. She remembered that night in her living room, and her fear was palpable. He walked around her, closing in tighter every time he circled, trapping her horror.

She wanted her doll for protection, but it had been shredded by the guards.

Stopping behind her, Crazy Eyes ran his fingers through her hair, and she tried to pull away, but she was confined.

"So lovely," Crazy Eyes said. He put his nose into the nape of her neck and sniffed long and deep, tonguing her skin to steal a taste. He caressed her cheek with cold fingers that made her shiver. "So, so lovely. You were the greatest prize I never had—or so I thought. How wrong I was."

"Come to me," Epiales said, and without delay Crazy Eyes walked back to him. "Go back from where you came. Her torment and this moment are mine."

Stacey watched between fingers she used to cover her eyes. Crazy Eyes stepped into the creature and disappeared.

"You," the beast said. His voice crawled on Stacey's skin like Crazy Eyes' touch. "Stand up."

The spindly fingers wrapped her hand, and with might, he encouraged her to stand. Her knees were weak, and her heart pounded inside her chest with such force she worried it would break out or explode.

"Why am I here?"

"Along with humility it seems you have many more lessons to learn. Now follow me."

Epiales turned and walked away, and as they left, amazingly, Stacey could see him with what little light shined underneath her door. She followed, trying to spy the place she was in while staying close. But the shadows held their secrets. Soon he stopped and turned to face her.

"Stand next to me," Epiales said, and Stacey did, still feeling the need to run but knowing that listening was her only option. "Face this way and reach your hand out and knock. There's someone you need to see."

Stacey reached a cautious hand out and felt the smooth cold surface of what felt like a metal door. As she knocked she heard the echo of the thump run away from her, and she wanted to follow the sound. It went someplace far away from here.

Moments later the hatch on the door slid open, and light beamed out of the hole. Stacey looked in and struggled against the impossible brightness but managed to see a young man approaching, holding something that drooped in his hands.

She looked behind herself and saw she was in a crypt of some sort. All around her in the room were coffins of all different sizes that were propped against the walls.

"Would you like to see who is inside them?" Epiales asked almost teasingly.

Stacey stepped closer to the door, trying to feel the heat and longing for the safety of the light. "No," she said. "Even in the light I'm scared, and I don't know why."

Spiderwebs hung from the ceiling, and the ground was of dirt. The rock wall was jagged and jutted outward like a thousand pointing fingers, accusing her of inhumane things.

"So you're the one who pushed me?" A voice said through the opening in the hatch. He spoke as if he knew her, but she didn't know him.

Stacey remained quiet for a moment. None of these things were making sense. "I didn't push you."

"Yes you did, and you almost killed me."

"When did I push you?"

"We were at the playground some years ago. You shoved me, and I fell. When we were kids. I broke my back."

"I didn't push you."

"Yes you did," the young man said with a bite to his tone. "You may not remember me, but you tried to kill me for reasons I'll never understand."

"How can you accuse me of such a thing when I know I've never met you before?"

"You met me. Although it may mean nothing to you now, my name is Beau. You were at the playground with your father and a doctor. Think on it. It may come to you."

Stacey shook her head. He was right, his name meant nothing to her, and neither did his claim of her having been with her father and a doctor. Her father left her. She remembered that right now.

"Forget it," Beau said. "You're so lost that I can't help you. I suppose that's why the others are here. But take this anyway—it may help you.

With what I learned about you, I can understand your confusion. You're going to have to give it back, so make sure you take care of him. It's very important to me and holds significant meaning."

Stacey watched the boy stuff through the hole a grimy grayish thing that had a long neck and legs. She took it and saw it was a stuffed giraffe. Mangy and pathetic, it dangled from her grasp. "His name is Rafi, and you are to take care of him. I'm not kidding. He's one of the most important things to me because he's helped me through some of the most terrible times of my life. He came back after he was left when he never should have been."

The plaything smelled foul—even in this tomb.

"By the time they're done with you, you will remember me and know what you are," the boy said. "I forgive you though because I don't think you can help it."

"Help what?"

"Whatever it is that you are. I just wish I could help you." He slammed the hatch closed, and with that the darkness came upon her again, and she pounded on the door in desperation.

"Please open up! I need the light."

"Even I know that," Epiales said and cackled. "But the light has no place in you."

# 19

# THE PACT

*The past.*

Deb exited the bathroom with an empty ice bucket and a phone to her ear. Stacey came out of her room at the same time.

"OK, Mom," Deb said and made sure the bathroom door was locked by jiggling the handle. "I will."

"Let me talk to her," Stacey said and grabbed for the phone.

"I said I will, Mom," Deb said and turned away, making Stacey miss. "OK, I'll talk to you later."

"Wait, I want to talk to her."

"OK. Bye."

Deb hung up the phone and walked down the stairs.

"I said I wanted to talk to her."

"She heard you and said she had to go. It sounded crazy busy at the diner, and I was having a hard time hearing her. She wanted me to tell you that she loves you and will call us sometime tomorrow after we get out of school. I told her about my having to go to the library so she said she would call a little later in the night. You can talk to her then."

"OK," Stacey said and followed her sister into the kitchen and watched her return the bucket to the freezer.

"I double checked the closets upstairs and underneath both our beds," Stacey said.

"Good. You're calm so I'm assuming you didn't find anything unusual or out of place?"

"No, I didn't," Stacey said and turned away. "But I would rather be safe than sorry."

"I understand, and I'm glad you're like that because you should be. You were right to want to look. I'd rather know we're safe in the house too. And the more I thought about it the more I knew looking around was the right thing for us to do."

"The bathroom?"

"Stinks like shit," Deb said and made a face. "Don't let Mom hear you say that word. I'm glad that the closed door is keeping the smell in there. We should put a couple of towels down at the bottom of the door so we don't get a back draft."

"I can do that."

"Good. And if Crazy Eyes was hiding out in there, the stink would've killed him."

Stacey giggled. "You still should've let me in there with you. You know, just in case."

"I assure you I saved you by not letting you in there. Taking care of that bathroom will be my job."

"OK."

"If you saw what was floating around in the standing water it'd make you sick. I had this idea to freeze lemon juice and dump it into the toilet, sink, and tub to help with the smell. It'll take a while for it to melt and should really help."

"You're very smart sometimes."

Deb smiled. "Dumping lemon flavored ice onto crap to help with the smell makes me smart?"

"No, it's not just that." Stacey drew a deep breath and sighed. "Your whole outlook is really smart. I'm sorry about before. I shouldn't have run out of the house like that. You were right. It was reckless and dumb, and I'll never do it again."

"I'm glad you've given it some thought. It shows you're maturing."

"But I want you to know I really like Larry, and all I was doing is what he's doing for me. I was looking out for him, and I thought I saw something and panicked."

"You've already told me that, and it's a very noble thing to do, Stacey," Deb said. "But as I said before we have to make sure we're protecting ourselves first. It is you and me against the world. I will never steer you wrong, and I'll make sure we make it through this together."

"I know you will, and I trust you with all of my heart. I also want you to understand that Larry just wants to be friends, and I'd like to have him as a friend."

"But I'm your friend."

"I know that," Stacey said. "But I'm talking about someone that's not my sister. Someone I can go out on the sidewalk with and have a catch and talk about stupid, meaningless things."

"Boys are trouble, Stacey."

"And if it were a girl?"

"I'd say they're catty and can't be trusted."

"I can't win."

"No, you can't. Not when it comes to anyone other than you and I sticking together as one. As long as you remember that's our pact everything will be fine."

# 20

# AWAKENING

*Present day.*

Stacey's head flopped forward, and she jerked awake. Drool ran out of her mouth, and confusion lingered in her mind like a thick fog. She sat up and wiped her mouth, and the foul odor of the stuffed animal she held onto filled her nose. The pain in her lower back was something that demanded her attention too.

"What the . . ."

She rubbed her eyes and saw the pink plastic thing she'd kicked beneath the door resting in her lap. She picked it up and tried to focus on it, not sure if it was real. Stuck in a moment of what was actual or a dream made her stand. Her knees buckled, but she used the wall to hold herself up. The question of how she actually collected the things she now possessed hit her like a closed fist punch from a 250 pound man.

"What is it, Marshmallow? You seem confused," Mara said.

Stacey looked at the things she held and then around the room.

"How did I end up here?"

"On the toilet?"

"Yes, on the toilet, in this room, with these things in my possession?" She held them up so Mara could see what they were.

"You either fell asleep or you blacked out. We were talking and you walked over to the door. You were acting weird and looked through the hatch, and you started to talk to someone that was out in the hallway."

"The guard, he was there."

"No he wasn't. I'm telling you it was really weird, Marshmallow. I'm not going to lie and tell you that you weren't freaking me out because it was the strangest thing ever."

Stacey shook her head. "The guard was out there. Only it wasn't the guard. He was like this black mist or shadow man or something. I could see his jagged teeth and smell his foul breath. He pulled me through the hatch and made me pick up this—" she showed Mara the pink piece of plastic—"and then brought me into this crypt where a young man or boy was in a cell much like this one. The boy gave me this." She held up the mangy stuffed animal.

"You must've had some dream because I picked you up off that floor myself and sat'cho scrawny ass on that bowl. I traded for that stuffed animal and got the plastic piece back too, and I put them in your lap."

"No," Stacey said. "The thing out in the hallway said he was the embodiment of a nightmare. He pulled me in through the slot in that door. He said his name was Epiales."

Mara smiled. "So he did come. Do you know who that is?"

"He said he was a nightmare demon or something like that."

"Yeah," Mara said with a smile. "Something like that. Remember I told you to sleep with one eye open."

Stacey's flesh goosed.

"Epiales is known in Greek mythology for being the nightmare spirit. I think you experienced a black dream." Mara looked at the slot in the door and pointed at it. "You're telling me he pulled you through that?"

"Yes, and I wasn't dreaming."

"Odd he would do that. Normally he would just lay on you as you sleep and enter your dreams," Mara said. "It seems he's created a nightmare world for you. Kind of like what I've done for you here."

"What do you mean he would lay on me and enter my dreams?"

"The sons of Nyx are the sons of night, and they cause people to have nightmares and do so by lying on their victims. If he didn't lay down on you, he created a special nightmare for you and took you inside it."

"He told me I got his attention and made him create nightmares and terror. He was angry that I did that. Could that be possible?"

"Yes. I already told you that you weren't a nice person, and you needed to learn humility."

"What in God's name did I do?"

"You killed people. Made some of them suffer. That's where Epiales comes in. Did you get to see what he looks like?"

"Like I said, I saw his mouth. He had jagged teeth, bad breath, and he had a terrible voice. When I went to the door and he made me listen to him, he had really strong spindly fingers that came in through the hatch and wrapped around my head. He pulled really hard, and my body collapsed in on itself to fit through that slot, and I came out normal on the other side."

"And what did you see on the other side?"

"A bitter darkness. But he was darker than the black he had me in. It was like he was a stain on the night. Then he brought me farther into the darkness, and I could see him better. His flat face, red eyes . . ."

"He allowed you to remember what he looked like?"

"So you didn't place those things in my lap?"

"I did."

"How did you get them?"

"What difference does it make, Marshmallow? I traded for them. They were pushed beneath the door. I'm telling you your physical body never left this room. Focus on that."

Stacey walked over to the sink where the dried-up flowers were and placed the pink plastic cylinder down and then set the dirty stuffed animal next to it. "I remember the young man I was telling you about accusing me of trying to kill him. He said his name was Beau, and that should mean something to me. It doesn't. This mangy looking thing belongs to him, and he told me how important it was to him, and then he reiterated it over again." Stacey fell into silence. Maybe if she stood there long enough and stared at it she'd be able to put the pieces of the puzzle together.

"You ain't seeing it yet, are you, Marshmallow?"

Stacey shook her head. "I have no idea what's going on, and now I'm frightened beyond words. I'm being accused of being a killer."

"That you are, and you should be scared because time is running short for you. I'm the one that invited Epiales, and I'm the one that asked him to show you the error of your ways."

"And who are you?"

"I'm a spirit guide."

"You talk to spirits?"

"No, I help the dead that cross over from trauma. I seek justice for the murdered."

Stacey laughed and Mara didn't.

"There is nothing funny about this."

"No," Stacey said, and her smile disappeared. "There's not. This Epiales brought me to a young man who accused me of doing terrible things to him. As hard as I try, I don't remember him. But I remember this child killer who haunted me when I was a kid. He came to taunt me from the shadows, and then the killer returned from where he came."

"I want you to know that he's doing exactly what I asked him to do. And I want you to know that he is not yet done with you. I told you I was going to break you, didn't I? That I didn't like you. Now you have some understanding as to why. Yet there is so much more to come."

# 21

# FRIENDS

*The past.*

"Thank you for walking me home again, Larry," Stacey said.

"You're welcome."

"I mean it," she said. "Thank you. I feel much safer having you around, knowing that you're looking out for me."

Larry looked at the ground, embarrassed.

"But mostly having you as a friend," she said. She'd never felt such sincerity.

"You're welcome, Stacey. I know you've got to get inside so I won't hang around feeling dumb because I don't know what to say. I'm not used to compliments from girls, especially ones as pretty as you. You have a good rest of your day."

He turned around, gave an awkward pause, and started to walk across the street toward his house.

"Larry, wait."

He stopped and looked over his shoulder.

"You're the first friend I've ever had, and I wanted you to know that."

"You're mine too. Kids in school have a tendency to either pick on me because of the color of my hair or ignore me. Either way, I don't have many people like you."

"I'm sorry they do that. How about we try and forget about the bad people and you come inside for a little while? We can play or just sit down and talk if you want."

"What happened to your not being allowed to have anyone over when your mother isn't home? I don't want to get you in any sort of trouble."

Stacey shrugged. "She's never home anyways, so what does it matter? Besides, I'm allowed to have friends, and that's what we are, right?"

"Right."

"So come inside for a little while."

"Are you sure?"

Stacey nodded. "Yes, I'm sure. I'll bet you we will have fun."

"OK, wait here, and let me check with my mom to make sure it's OK."

Stacey watched Larry run across the street and disappear through his front door, hollering for his mother as he did so.

Stacey took the opportunity to make sure Deb was at the library and their mother hadn't come home.

"Deb? Mom?" she called into the house and was relieved when she didn't get a response.

There was a knock on the front door, and Stacey saw Larry peering through the screen the same way Crazy Eyes had. But Larry wasn't creepy. "My mom said I can play with you until dinnertime."

"That's great. Come on in," Stacey said.

Larry entered and looked around.

"So, this is my house. What do you think?"

"It's nice."

"Thank you. Why don't we go upstairs so I can show you my room?"

Stacey led Larry up the stairs and toward her room. She pointed at the closed bathroom door as they walked by. "If you need to go, you'll have to use the bathroom downstairs because this one is broken."

"OK," Larry said and followed Stacey into her small but neat bedroom.

"If you pull the curtain back, you can see what I see when I'm checking up on you."

Larry did. "So who do you think this killer is?"

Stacey shrugged her shoulders. "I don't know."

"I think it's a middle-aged white man, and he probably has a family of his own or he comes from a broken home."

Larry's words held her interest. "Why do you say that?"

"Because most serial killers are white, and I think there's a balance somewhere between them living a double life or being completely out of control. And even the ones that are out of control are smart."

"I hope he's not too smart," Stacey said. She sat on her bed and watched Larry as he continued to look out her window. His stare was intense, and she wondered what he was looking at. "I hope he makes a mistake."

"Well whoever he is, he's not smarter than the police. He'll slip up, and they'll catch him." He looked at her. "They always do. You'll see."

"Maybe it's a she and not a he?"

"No."

"Why not?"

"The killings required strength. I don't think a woman could do that. It just doesn't fit."

"You say things with such confidence."

"My mom and dad watch this television show where the police have forty-eight hours to catch a killer using the clues and eyewitness testimony. I love it, and I want to be a criminologist when I grow up. I like trying to profile people."

"Oh yeah?" Stacey said with a big smile. "Profile me."

Larry rubbed his chin and resigned with a smile. "You're shy but smart. Scared, but there is a braveness deep down inside that will come out one day. It's the type that will make a difference in your life. It's like you'll take a stand for yourself or something."

"Stacey?" a voice called from downstairs.

*Thump. Thump. Thump.*

That was her sister, and she was coming up the stairs. Stacey had gotten so wrapped up in what Larry was saying that she didn't even hear her come in the door. She thought she was staying at school late today to go to the library.

"Please, Larry, hide in the closet, will you?"

"What for? Is everything OK?"

"Yes, everything will be fine. But for now, please do as I ask."

Stacey stepped out of her room and met Deb on the top step.

"What are you doing?" Deb said. "You had me worried. I was calling your name and you weren't answering me."

"I was in my room with the door shut. I think I might have gotten what you had yesterday." She rubbed her stomach. "I'm just laying down for a while."

"Can I get you anything?" Deb said.

"No, I'm fine. I'm just a little tired I guess."

"Did you crack the ice when you got home?"

"No," Stacey said. "The way I was feeling, it totally slipped my mind."

"That is the type of stuff you can't just forget," Deb said. "I can't do my job if you don't do yours. And you still haven't put the towels down in front of the door. I don't want that smell getting out."

"I know it's important, but I needed to lay down."

"I understand, but do you think you can get those things done for me sooner than later?"

"Yes," Stacey said. "Let me lay down for a little while longer, and I'll go take care of the ice and I'll do the towels. I promise."

"OK," Deb said and disappeared down the hall, going into her own room. "I'm going to lay down for a little while before I start on dinner and we move onto doing our homework. I'm still not fully recovered myself. Maybe it's a bug or something."

"I thought you said you were going to the library after school today?"

"I was, but like you, I'm still not feeling good. I figured it can wait until another day."

"Is there anything I can do to help you?"

"No, Stacey, but thank you. Just keep making that ice like I've been asking and get them towels down. I just need to get off of my feet for a little while and maybe get changed. I'm tired today."

"OK," Stacey said and opened her bedroom door just wide enough for her to fit through. "I'll see you downstairs in a half hour or so."

"Try not to fall asleep," Deb said. "We did that last night, and things didn't go too well after we got up."

"Don't worry. That won't happen again."

Deb stepped inside her room and closed the door, and that prompted Stacey to close her door too.

"OK, you can come out now," she said to Larry.

Larry stepped out of the closet. "Who were you talking to?"

"No one. It doesn't matter. Don't worry about it."

"OK," Larry said. He seemed to get lost within himself for a moment. "Whoever it was, they're not cool about my being in here, are they?"

Stacey shook her head. "No, not at all."

"What did you say?"

"That I wasn't feeling well and I was lying down."

"Why didn't you tell them the truth?"

"Look, it's really complicated. First, you're a boy in my room, and I'm sure you can understand how this might look."

"But we're just friends."

"I know that. We know that, but like I said, you can understand how this might look."

"I suppose. But I don't see any harm in us being friends."

"Me either," Stacey said. "Look, it's more than that. It's like I said. It's complicated . . . I'm complicated because I'm always being told to keep to myself. I took a big step by hanging out with you and taking to you so fast."

"Why?"

"Because that's the way it has always been. I never really thought to question it because that's the way it is."

"Well maybe you should question it."

"Like I said, it's complicated." She felt a surge of frustration threaten to bubble to the surface. "When the time is right, I suppose I will, but now is not the time. I already spoke about you and how I'd like to be your friend."

"That's good," Larry said and neared Stacey. "What did they say?"

"To be careful. To not place too much trust in you. They don't trust you the same way your father doesn't trust me."

"Trust is all I can offer you if we're going to be friends and look out for each other. I don't care what my father says, and I haven't done anything wrong for whoever was out there in the hall not to trust me."

"Neither did I." But she knew that wasn't true. She was a liar and a killer. Her eyes roamed around the room as she tried to figure out a way to explain the dynamics of her family without giving away too much.

"Since my stepdad died, Mom's been out of the house a lot, and I have to be careful is all."

"I understand," Larry said and drew Stacey's eyes to his own. "And I don't blame anyone for being protective of you. You're a good person, Stacey, and your being home alone is dangerous. That's why I wanted to watch over you."

Stacey smiled. "Thank you for that, but I'll be fine. I have to get you out of here without anyone knowing."

"Tell me what to do, and I'll do it. I'll prove to you my friendship is real. I don't want to cause you any trouble."

"All I need you to do is to keep quiet and follow me out of the house. Can you do that?"

"Of course I can."

# 22

# THE LETTER

*Present day.*

"Hey, Marshmallow," Mara said. "You've been standing there staring at those things for over an hour. Why don't you give up?"

"Because you've gone through an awful lot of trouble to get me these things, and it's supposed to mean something to me. Besides, that demon thing that walked me through that nightmare has left me with the feeling of a million things crawling on my skin." She shivered. "I want to know what this is about and stay as far away from it as I can."

"You do understand that what you're looking at is a complex puzzle. And you, Marshmallow, are a piece within the puzzle too. So don't over-look that. You also need to know that there are pieces that are missing that could never be brought in on a tray or torn into pieces and thrown down at your feet. It's impossible."

"Oh, so that was a part of this puzzle as well. So what's the point in going through the trouble?" Stacey said and faced Mara. "Why punish me, belittle me to the point where I'm afraid of you and this place, and all I can do is cry because I'm stuck in a never-ending cycle? Now you make it seem as though you're trying to help me, but yet I feel like you're saying that you really can't?"

"I'm not trying to help you. I'm trying to help them."

"Them?"

"The people you killed. I'm advocating for you to release their souls. The pieces you are missing are vital to knowing who you are and require you going back out into that nightmare. Then and only then can things start to make sense. Are you willing to do that?"

She shivered. "I don't like it out there."

"Is it any worse than what I'm putting you through in here?"

She weighed the two options, and although she wanted to get back in the room with Mara when she was out there, she understood that it wasn't that much different in here. The light and the dark were the same and she wants out of both of them in the worst way.

"No, it's not."

"So what do you have to lose?"

"Nothing." She let out a nervous laugh. "Maybe it'll give me a chance to escape the abuse."

"You'll be able to escape the abuse I will continue to put you through inside this room, yes. But the hell you've made for yourself is and always will be your cross to bear. I cannot and would not take that away from you. That would be unfair to those that have suffered at your hands."

Mara stepped on the bottom bunk and reached onto the top. She came down with an envelope in one hand and something small in the other that Stacey couldn't make out. Mara turned and handed it to Stacey. "There's your letter, and here, this was also inside the envelope." Mara handed her a broken toothpick. "Hold onto them both for now, but go on and read your letter while you have the chance."

Stacey took the letter, and her anger and frustration were gone in an instant. A tremble entered her hand as she read the return address again and verified it was indeed from home. She reached a hand inside and withdrew the neatly folded paper and opened it up, careful not to rip the page. A dollar bill fell out of the unfolded pages and twirled as it fell to the floor, captivating Stacey into a deeper curiosity.

Fancy dips and swirls from the hand of a woman confirmed to Stacey that Deb had written the letter within as well.

*Remember, no matter what you do, don't tell them anything. They're only going to try and pull us apart.*

That was it? She looked at Mara and noticed she had taken to the bottom bunk and had her hands behind her head and her eyes were closed.

The tattoos on the backs of her eyes were creepy and appeared to be looking at her.

Stacey picked up the dollar bill and noted how it was crumpled and damp. She was confused as to how it didn't wet the paper. It seemed as though anything was possible in this weird place.

"What's this supposed to mean?"

Mara opened one eye and looked at Stacey. She stared at her for a long while. "I don't know, why don't you tell me?"

"How am I supposed to know?"

"Well that's what came for you, and that's why I didn't want to give it to you. I knew you weren't ready for it. I didn't think you'd ever be ready for it."

Stacey plopped herself down at the foot of the bunk and hung her head. A swell of emotion bulged in her chest and started to move into her face.

"Get off my rack," Mara said.

Stacey cried, ignoring Mara's hard demand.

"Hey, Marshmallow!"

Stacey stopped crying, sat up straight, and looked at Mara with unabashed anger. "Stop calling me that!"

Mara swung a leg and swept Stacey onto the floor. She got up and looked down on her. "I told you thatchu ain't allowed on the damn bunks. You wanna cry? Go ahead and cry but go sit yo' ass on yo' seat and do it over there. Now get off my damn floor, ya big baby."

Mara sat back down and slowly reclined into a lying position.

"Don't you be thinking I've been tampering with yo' letter 'cause I didn't! It's just another damn piece of the puzzle that makes up your life, and it's in fragments. Just like that thinkin' of yours."

"But why?"

"Because that's the way you made it. Just like you weren't placed in this room with me by accident. I am here to break your will. Dismantle you in any way possible. I gotchu now, don't I?"

Stacey moved to her feet, took the letter and the dollar bill, and set them next to her other trinkets. She looked at them one at a time, trying to make some sense of their meaninglessness. Then she remembered being handed the broken toothpick. She looked on the floor where Mara had pushed her, and it was there. She picked it up and looked at it. Although it was broken, it was still attached, splintered and tilted at an awkward angle. This item made even less sense to her.

"You're right. I can't do this anymore. My head hurts as bad as my back, and we're only going around in circles." Stacey sat on the bowl and dug her fists into her eyes.

Mara sat up. "Now you're ready for answers?"

"When will I get them?"

"I'll give them to you starting right now. Open your hand."

She did and showed Mara the toothpick.

"What that toothpick represents is on its way right now. We will start with the piece you're holding. Brace yourself—this ain't gonna be easy."

"What's coming for me?"

"Only more nightmares . . ."

# 23

# YOU HAD IT ALL WRONG

*The past.*

"Stay close behind me and walk as quietly as you can," Stacey said, and Larry nodded. There was a palpable thickness in the air from the nervousness between the two of them.

"Are you ready?"

"Yes," he said and blew out a strong breath.

She pulled her bedroom door open a crack and spied the hallway. Everything was clear, and Deb's bedroom door remained closed.

"OK," she said and looked over her shoulder. "We better move fast, but remember to be quiet."

Stacey went to pull the door open fully when she saw someone step into the hallway, exiting the locked bathroom. A knot formed in the pit of her stomach, and a wave of panic came over her. She closed her door as quietly as she could and leaned her back against it. Her eyes were wide and she gasped for air.

"What is it?" Larry said, her concern becoming his own. He reached out and touched her arm. "Stacey?"

"I . . . I don't know." She placed a trembling hand over her heart.

"What do you mean you don't know? What did you see?"

She bent at the knees and tried to gulp some air. "I'm not sure if I saw who I think I saw." She panted some more, this time drawing some breath. "I need to calm down and think this through. My heart feels like it's gonna pound out of my chest. And I can't really breathe."

"I think you're having a panic attack. You look like you've seen a ghost, and you're shaking so much that you're scaring me. Your face is as white as paper, and you don't even look like you should be upright at all."

She licked her lips, and her spit was like glue. "What I might have seen is something far worse than a ghost," she said. But what she saw didn't make sense. Maybe her mind was playing tricks on her.

"What is it? Please talk to me," Larry said.

"I don't feel good."

"What did you see? You're really freaking me out."

"I'm not sure," Stacey said and swallowed hard. She moved in silence and fought against all the things that were wrong inside her body. Opening the door a pinch, she looked into the hallway again. Sure enough, Crazy Eyes was in the hallway with his back to her.

Stacey's eyes bulged as she tried to understand why he was just standing there. She watched him walk quietly into Deb's room and close the door behind himself.

"The killer is in the house," she whispered. She had just seen him for the second time, and that reaffirmed what she saw. "The killer is in the house right now."

"He's in the house?"

"Yes! I just saw him standing in the hallway."

Larry pushed the door closed carefully so it didn't make a sound. "Wait. Slow down a second. Calm down."

"Don't tell me to calm down! I just saw the killer standing five feet outside this door!" she whispered frantically.

"Is this a joke?"

"Does it look like I'm joking? The killer, the guy that killed our friends and dumped their bodies in the forest is here."

"How do you know it's him?"

"That night Tammy was taken, I saw the killer."

"You what?"

"He came to my door and tried to lure me outside. I called for Deb, and I assume he thought I said dad, and he fled into the night."

"Who is Deb?"

"She's my older sister."

"I didn't know you had a sister."

"Who did you think she was this whole time, my mother?"

"Think who was?" Larry's face showed his confusion.

"My sister."

Larry shrugged, and Stacey stared at him, put off by his sudden odd behavior.

"Are you doing this to scare me? Because if you are, you're doing a really good job of it," Larry said. "Why didn't you tell me you saw the killer before?"

"Because I figured if I ignored it, it would just go away. Besides, would you have believed me?"

"Yes I would have believed you. Knowing you saw him just before the killings has to be eating you up inside. No wonder you panicked yesterday and thought he was outside my house."

"That was an honest mistake. Your dad was wearing the same clothes as the killer."

"My dad's not the killer."

"I know that. I saw the man's face. He had these strange eyes that looked in different directions. It has been an awful secret, and I've had nightmares almost every night, and I'm so afraid of the dark it feels alive to me. I'm afraid of who is around me, and I'm afraid to be alone."

"You should have gone to the police."

"I should have but didn't. I was scared, and it is like I said: I figured if I kept quiet, he'd leave me alone."

"Are you sure you saw him?"

"I'm positive," Stacey said.

"Out in the hallway?"

"Yes! Please don't ask again because it's like you don't believe me. I saw him then, and I just saw him now. He went into my sister's room. I watched him with my own two eyes."

"Well we have to get out of here," Larry said. "We have to go for help."

Stacey just stood there. Thoughts of what that maniac might be doing to her sister made her stomach queasy. Larry's advice was lost in her own mental state of anxiety making her indecisive and irrational.

"I've got to get her out of that room."

"You can't do that," Larry said and tugged on her shirt. "Let's go."

"I can't just leave her."

"Yes you can if you want to help her. We need to get out of here and call the police. If we hope to catch this killer, then we better move fast. You going in there to confront him helps no one."

Stacey nodded and remembered Deb's instructions. She needed to be smart and think ahead. Everything Larry was saying made the most sense. "OK, let's do this."

She cracked the door open again. No one was there, and everything was quiet. "Come on," she whispered and tiptoed into the hallway and watched her sister's door. She stayed close to the wall and made her way to the stairs. Larry remained close behind her, matching her footfall step for step, careful in every placement, as quiet as a mouse.

Just then Deb's bedroom door opened, and Deb stepped into the hallway. She was looking down at her feet, talking out loud to herself. "I've got to do something about that bathroom. It's starting to smell," she said and looked up and saw Stacey and Larry. Her face distorted into something very angry and ugly. "What's this?" Deb said. Her voice boomed.

"Shh, he's going to hear you and come out," Stacey said. "We're going for help."

"What the hell are you talking about?"

"What are you doing?" Larry said.

"Hush," Stacey said to Larry and stared at her sister, her confusion only deepening by her outrage. Her sister had to see Crazy Eyes enter the room. That is, unless she had fallen asleep and just woke up and he hid in a closet or something.

"What is he doing in our house?" Deb said, pointing at Larry.

"Don't worry about him. He's not the problem. Listen to me, I saw Crazy Eyes go into your room," Stacey said. "How did you not see him? He had to walk right by you."

"Never mind what you think you saw. I asked you what Larry is doing in our house." Deb's eyes were wide with the question, a wild look about her face, and her voice grew shrill.

"I've gotta go," Larry said.

"You're not going anywhere!" Deb said.

"Didn't you hear what I said? Crazy Eyes walked into your room, and we need to get out of here!"

"I heard you, but did you hear me?" She took a step toward Stacey. "What is Larry doing here? Answer my damn question."

"I just wanted a friend to hang out with, that's all. He's leaving."

"I'm really freaking out, Stacey. Who are you talking to?" Larry said.

"And I told you to stay away from him! I told you we had to protect ourselves and stick together, but you didn't listen!"

Stacey started to cry. She'd never seen her sister so mad at her.

"What do you know?" Deb said to Larry.

Larry remained stiff and afraid. "You're still really scaring me, and I want to get out of here."

"He should be scared because he knows and that can't be. Listen to my words, Stacey. He knows exactly what's going on." She turned her eyes to Stacey. "Now what did you tell him you saw?"

"That Crazy Eyes went into your room. I told him he was the one that killed Tammy and Jake on the path."

"You see? This is why I told you that it is just you and I. Boys are trouble! But you didn't listen, and now look at the problem we have."

"I don't understand what's happening," Larry said. His body was stiff and his eyes widened by his outward fear. "I just want to get out of here!"

"You invited someone into our house that shouldn't be here, and I'm afraid of what else he might know."

"Get out now, Larry. Go!" Stacey said.

Larry shimmied around Stacey, pressing his back against the wall, his eyes fixed on her.

"He knows too much."

"What are you saying?"

"That we can't let him leave."

Larry made a break for it. He rushed past Deb and flew down the steps two at a time. Deb's bedroom door swung open and Crazy Eyes immediately plunged down the steps and caught Larry before he reached the bottom step.

"Help—"

"Shut the hell up!"

Crazy Eyes slapped a hand over Larry's mouth, stifling a scream that might get the attention of a neighborhood already on edge.

"What are you going to do with him?" Stacey shouted. She looked at Deb. "Why is that lunatic in our house, and why does he seem to be helping you?"

"Shut your mouth, and let us deal with one problem at a time." She turned to Crazy Eyes. "Bring him up here."

Crazy Eyes started to drag Larry up the steps, and Larry struggled, fighting to escape the powerful hands that restrained him.

"You've ruined it all," Deb said. "You should have listened, but you couldn't do that, could you? You couldn't follow simple instructions, and now this is going to get ugly."

Stacey had no words.

"You're going to see what Crazy Eyes is doing here and why I kept telling you to ignore the boy." Deb shook her head. "But you just wouldn't listen!"

"You're scaring me, Deb. What is this about?"

"That if he gets away then people will find out."

"Find out about what?"

"All of our secrets, Stacey. We have to protect our secrets, and there are a lot of them. You know that pocket that's stuffed with all the bad things you've done? People are going to know about it and open it up."

# 24

# TRUTH WITHIN A NIGHTMARE

*Present day.*

Mara pushed the hatch open and shouted into it. "Bring him over and open the door. I'm about done with this one."

Stacey watched Mara stand and place her hands behind her back. She rocked on her heels, and the heavy door clicked and slid open. What was supposed to be a brightly lit hallway was a dark, uninviting maw of oppression and heaviness. It had all the characteristics of her nightmare.

A gurney was pushed in front of the opening, and Stacey could only see the lower half of what she perceived to be a body covered with a sheet. She craned her neck and shifted on her feet to get a better look, but the darkness wanted to keep its secrets for the moment.

"Come over here, Marshmallow, and bring what you're holding," Mara said.

Stacey looked at the splintered toothpick and twirled it between her pointer finger and thumb. She walked toward the gurney, and anxiety shook her limbs and dried her mouth.

"Look at what you're holding and compare it to what you see. Then I want you to give what you hold to the person in the bed," Mara said.

Stacey stepped one foot into the hallway, and a strong feeling repelled her and she reeled. She bounced off of Mara, who had moved behind her, keeping her from being able to flee.

"Stacey," the man on the gurney said, lying on his side, his voice rife with pain.

Stacey didn't recognize his voice but somehow knew she should. She was afraid but wasn't sure of what exactly.

"I didn't do anything to your mother, and you know it," he said. "It was all in your head, and you did this to me. All because you were angry that your father had left you, and you blamed me for it."

His voice was weak and conveyed little meaning to Stacey. The words he struggled so hard to speak hit her in the head and fell at her feet.

"I want you to pull back the sheet and look at what you've done," Mara said.

Stacey reached out a hand, grasped the sheet, and pulled it down. She flinched at what she saw and turned away.

"Oh God," she said.

"No, no, Marshmallow," Mara said. "You hold up the thing in your hand and look at him good. Compare the two and tell me what they have to do with each other."

She held up the toothpick and then looked at him. Bent and broken somewhere in the middle of his spine, his body shape mimicked the toothpick exactly. "It's broken like his back."

"Yes, it is. You did that when you pushed him down a flight of stairs," Mara said. "Not because he was an abusive stepfather or a drunk. You did it because you were angry and wanted to. Now give it to him so he can go in peace, knowing there was nothing he did wrong to deserve what happened to him."

Stacey placed the broken toothpick down next to the man's head and quickly moved away.

"Now go to the sink and look your items over."

Stacey stood in front of the shelf, shaken by what she just saw. She looked at the letter, the stuffed animal, the pink plastic thing, the dead flowers, and the dollar bill. She looked over her shoulder and was relieved that the gurney was gone. The blackened hallway remained, and it made her whimper because she knew there were more monsters out there she'd have to face.

"Now take dem off the shelf and hold onto 'em. Every piece you gathered. We're going on a little trip."

"Where are we going?"

"To seek the truth you want. We're going to finish putting the puzzle together so I can get you outta my hair. You make me sick."

Stacey gathered the items, her shaking hands full and a bit clumsy.

"You're consumed with fear and confusion, Marshmallow, when you should be filled with regret. Follow me," Mara said and exited the room. Stacey hurried to stay by her side. They walked straight ahead, using the light coming from their cell, and stopped at the cell across the way from them.

"What happened to the man with the broken back?"

"That was your stepfather, Stacey. He's moved on finally because he was able to get closure. He was just an innocent victim of your dysfunction and didn't deserve what happened to him."

Mara knocked on the steel door. "Now I want you to focus on what is in front of you. It is time, and I will be relieved to be rid of your burdens once and for all," she said and took a step back.

Stacey watched the door slide open, and standing in the doorway was a young boy. He was missing his nose and his upper lip. His top teeth were exposed, and his breathing was labored and made a sick bubbling sound.

"Give him what belongs to him," Mara said. "Set him free."

Stacey shuffled through the items and found the dried bouquet and handed it to him. She didn't know why she chose that item to give to him, but it felt right. The boy began to cry.

"Come with us, Jake. Stay with me now, and I will take you where you need to be. Your time here is done," Mara said. "And don't you worry about her. She can't hurt you anymore."

Guilt for the boy's sorrow and scarring choked Stacey up, but she didn't know why. Mara turned around and walked through the dim hallway, going to a door that was adjacent to her own cell, giving her no time to dwell in the moment.

Mara knocked on the door. "Come, Tammy, your time here is done."

The door slid open, and a young girl stood there. Her white nightgown was stained with dirt. She was clearly timid and afraid, and Jake stepped forward and took her hand.

"Everything is going to be all right," he said, his open wounds still bleeding and hard to look at. Tammy took Jake's hand despite what he looked like. She looked at Stacey with trepidation and fright.

"You see how she looks at you?" Mara said. "There's a reason for that."

Stacey noticed what appeared to be burn marks on the girl's wrists and bruising around her neck.

"Go on, give her what belongs to her," Mara said. "She can't leave until you set her free."

Without hesitation, Stacey handed her the pink plastic thing.

"Do you remember anything yet?" Mara said to Stacey.

Stacey shook her head.

"Then explain how you know what to give them."

"I can't," Stacey said. "But yet somehow I know. It's a feeling I can't explain." She rubbed her head.

Mara pulled at her chin. "Epiales is behind you. He will remind you then. No matter how you suffer, it will be nothing compared to theirs. That is another reason why I hate you. Remember that as he descends upon you. Don't look, children, turn away."

Stacey turned around and saw the black stain standing so close she could feel a pulse of cold air emanating from it. She dropped the things she held and moved backward only to trip. Falling hard, she hit her head on the firm ground and saw stars. When she came to, she could feel something crawling up her legs and latching onto her with tight fingers that reminded her of cat's claws but much longer. She wanted to scream at what she saw and felt but couldn't produce a sound. She watched as the monster clawed its way up her body and sat on her chest. It was ugly, this thing, no longer cloaked by the blackness, and she was paralyzed by it. She watched the beast lower himself and lie on top of her. With his spindly hands, he pried her clenched teeth open and breathed into her mouth.

Stacey found herself in a forest. Last she remembered she was at home, trembling with fear over the man with the crazy eyes who'd tried to lure her outside. Yet here she was with a girl just about her age lying limp in her arms. She was strong enough to hold her without strain. The young girl's arms were tied behind her back with a jump rope, and her neck looked blackish in the pale moonlight. It only made sense that hands had wrapped the girl's throat and squeezed with all of their crushing might. The killer must have been frenzied with rage.

Sickened by what she saw, she dumped the lifeless body in a cluster of foliage and ran toward home. She hoped her sister didn't know she had left the house without telling her.

"Stand up," Mara said. "Your lesson is far from over."

Stacey felt foggy in the head and unsure of what she just experienced. She stood and turned fast, looking all around, searching for Epiales.

"He's gone for now, but he's not done with you," Mara said. "Lessons, Marshmallow. I need to collect my dead, and they've waited long enough on your behalf." Mara's voice went soft. "Now come, children, stay close to me. I'll protect you." She looked at Stacey, and her tone of voice was harsh again. "Pick up the things you dropped, Marshmallow, and follow us."

They walked to the end of the corridor where all the coffins leaned against the wall, and Mara knocked on another steel door. The door opened, and the young man Stacey had seen before was standing there, undaunted, waiting.

"Now give him what belongs to him," Mara said.

Stacey handed him the mangy giraffe, and the boy hugged it and took a step back into the cell.

"Did you take care of him?" the young man asked.

Stacey nodded. "I think so."

He looked at Mara. "She has no idea, does she?"

Mara shook her head. "Not a clue."

"What a shame."

"At least you have been spared her wrath," Mara said. "One of the very few that has stepped into her path and survived. Sariel shows you favor, and that is good. You must have something important left to do yet or you wouldn't have lived."

"I know what it is and I think you do too," Beau said, and the metal door closed.

"We must move on," Mara said and ascended an uneven stone staircase hidden by the shadows. Mara moved Stacey to the front. "Take us to the top."

Once they reached the top, Stacey stared at a door that allowed light to seep out all around it. There was a doorknob, and it almost begged her to turn it.

Spindly fingers slowly wrapped Stacey's face, and she tried to resist, but the hands were too strong. She struggled but couldn't see, and the voice, although disturbing, was calm.

"Shh," Epiales said and emerged from the shadows. "You cannot escape all that must be seen." The beast appraised her.

Stacey relaxed. There was no sense in fighting. She couldn't win. That's why she submitted to Mara and now to Epiales. Maybe she was learning humility.

"Good, now find the handle and open the door."

She did, and twisted the knob, and gave the door a push. The hands that wrapped her let her go and took the envelope and dollar bill. He nudged her forward.

Stacey's mother was in the bathtub, relaxing with her eyes closed, her breathing slow and even.

"Mom?" she said.

Her mother's eyes snapped open. "What is it, Stacey?"

"I'm not sure." She looked over her shoulder and saw a plain wall. "I forgot why I came in here."

Her mother was mad, and she didn't attempt to hide it. "Are you kidding me right now?"

Stacey just stood there, not knowing what to say or how to take her mother's reaction to her presence.

"I work my fingers to the bone, and I asked you for a half hour of peace and quiet, and you can't even respect that?"

"I just wanted to ask you something."

"What is it then?"

"I can't remember now."

"Get the hell out! You have no respect for my privacy. I swear there are times I wish your father would've taken you with him!"

Stacey exited the bathroom and found herself walking downstairs, through the house, and out the back door. She was there but wasn't in control of her thoughts or actions. It was as if something else had taken over and she was on autopilot.

Picking up bricks used as trimming for the backyard rock garden, she carried as many as she could through the house and up the stairs, setting them down in a neat stack outside the bathroom door. She repeated the trip many more times without knowing why.

# 25

# THE REAL ARRIVAL

*The past.*
*Sixty minutes ago.*

With a nervous heart, Stacey approached a woman in a sterile room. The woman was sitting alone behind a desk and working hard. When Stacey drew near, the woman behind the desk looked up at her with a big smile and said, "Hello, you must be Margaret Gerner."

Stacey smiled nervously and nodded her head.

"Oh you poor thing, don't worry yourself too much. I've been in that room before, and although I didn't last too long, I don't think there's anything to be nervous about." The woman shuffled through desk drawers and gathered papers as she moved about. "Don't get me wrong, some weird trippy things happen that you can't readily explain away, but you're completely safe."

The heavy beat of Stacey's heart and the sweat on the palms of her hands were signs of her nerves. She shifted from foot to foot, looking at the woman, trying to understand the things she was explaining.

She raised a brow and smiled at Stacey. "Anything for science, huh?"

Stacey smiled again and wiped her hands on her pajama pants.

"I'm glad you came casual, but I don't think you'll be inside there that long. A pen and paper isn't recommended for you to take in the room. You'll be able to take notes on your experiences, but it should wait until you are out of the chamber. We don't want anything in there that might stimulate you."

Stacey mindlessly nodded.

"If you need to use the restroom I suggest you do so now."

Stacey just stood there, listening, intrigued by the woman. She didn't have to use the restroom so she just remained.

"Before we begin, Margaret, I have some papers I need you to look over and sign," the woman said as she placed the papers on a clipboard and handed Stacey a pen. "You can have a seat anywhere you want. Take your time in reading over every page of the consent, and initial the bottom of each page. If you have any questions, I'll be right here for you. Once you're done going through the consent forms we'll get started immediately. We know that sitting and waiting can allow your nerves to get the better of you. We want this to be an experience you don't forget anytime soon, and it spills into an accurate report for your viewers to see."

Stacey took the clipboard and sat in the closest seat. Skimming the pages, she pretended to know how to read. After a quick moment, she scribbled on each page with a sloppy hand and brought the clipboard up to the desk.

"Are you sure you don't want to go over these papers a bit more thoroughly?"

Stacey shook her head.

"You understand that hallucinations and panic are a part of sensory deprivation?"

Stacey nodded and tried to form a word, but something inside paralyzed her vocal chords. She ran her fingers through her hair, and the woman behind the desk shrugged her shoulders.

"OK. I wish you luck, and I'll see you when you get out. I'm looking forward to seeing your report on the television."

The woman behind the desk picked up the phone. "Please send Dubreuil in. Mrs. Gerner has arrived and is ready to enter the chamber."

Less than a minute went by before a man dressed in a long white doctor's smock emerged from a door Stacey hadn't noticed. He extended his hand. "Hello, Mrs. Gerner, I'm Doctor Dubreuil. I'm thrilled you decided to cover sensory deprivation. It is an interesting subject that has been mostly ignored and I believe what you're doing will create some buzz in the field.

I believe studying the human mind in situations such as this is paramount. Indeed you reporters have a fascinating job. I want you to know I'll be with you and monitoring you during your stay here."

Stacey looked at the doctor's hand and couldn't imagine what it must be like to extend an act of kindness. She merely stared at his hand, unable to shake it.

"She went over the contract?" the doctor asked and withdrew his hand. He looked at the woman behind the desk.

"She's all set."

"Very well," the doctor said and looked at Stacey. "Any questions before we get started?"

Stacey shook her head, nervous but eager to get started on whatever this was.

"OK then, follow me," he said and walked to a door at the far end of the room. "At any time you're uncomfortable you tell me and we will stop."

Stacey nodded her understanding. Excitement bubbled up inside her for the first time in years, and she wanted to do this in the worst way and began to shake. It wasn't nerves anymore and certainly not trepidation. It was a necessity to know what it was like.

Through the door and all the way at the end of a dimly lit hallway was another door. It was raw steel and looked like it was the entrance to an impenetrable bunker. She walked toward it without reservation, determined to identify and ultimately rid herself of what plagued her. She was lucky this Margaret Gerner didn't show up for her appointment. Otherwise who knows what would have happened in her discovery of the possibility of perfect silence. Perhaps she would have thrown herself from a tall bridge or building, or maybe step into the path of an oncoming vehicle. That would silence her misery. But yet somehow she was here. Guided by something unseen. It seemed fate had plans for her—or maybe it was chance?

Doctor Dubreuil unlocked the metal door and gave it a mighty tug. It swung open slowly, and what Stacey saw was amazingly beautiful, and it took her breath away. The walls had board-like objects sticking out of them in a V shape—one horizontal, the other vertical—and the pattern repeated itself over and over again covering every inch of the wall. A single chair positioned in the rear portion of the room caught her attention. The floor was made of a strong mesh net.

"Please," Doctor Dubreuil said. "Go on inside and make yourself as comfortable as possible in that chair and be as still as you can. Once you're settled we will allow you to begin the experiment."

Stacey entered the room, and though there was a slight spring to her footsteps, the net floor was firm and kept her advancement completely quiet.

"Do you see this red button here?" Doctor Dubreuil asked and knocked on the wall beside the door. Stacey looked, and there was a red button next to the door. "When you need to get out, press this button, and I will come and get you. Please keep in mind it takes me about fifteen seconds to open the door. I'll be monitoring you from a different room using closed-circuit cameras. Enjoy your time inside the anechoic chamber."

The doctor closed the door with a smile, and the last thing Stacey heard was the lock on the door slide into place.

Somehow she had found peace at last.

# 26

# MANY ARE ONE

*The past.*

Stacey opened the bathroom door and allowed it to swing until it banged into the wall. Her mother stood at the sink and looked into the mirror while she brushed her hair. She turned around and looked at Stacey standing in the doorway. Disappointment covered her face, and she sighed, her hands going to her hips.

"Did you know you should probably knock first?" her mother said. There was a bite to her tone, and Stacey's demeanor changed behind a smile she tried to conceal. "The bathroom is a place of privacy, and you constantly seem to forget that. I'm entitled to my privacy. What if I was using the toilet?"

"I knocked, but you didn't answer me." She approached her mother, and amidst the makeup and hairspray, Stacey spotted a dollar bill and took it. She put it in her pocket.

"What are you doing?" her mother said.

"I wanted to ask you something."

"I'm not talking about that. I'm talking about the money you just took and put in your pocket."

"What about it?"

"That's not yours, it's mine. I went to work and earned it. What you just did is considered stealing."

"It's a dollar, Mom. I figured maybe I could get myself a candy bar."

"You could ask."

"And you would've said no."

"Give it back."

"No. I'm not going to give it back because you ignored me when I was knocking at the door. Why should I listen to you?"

"Maybe I didn't answer you for a reason. Did you ever think of that?"

"Well if you don't answer me how do I know you even heard me?"

"You don't. But somehow you think that's an invitation to come in and invade my privacy and take my money?"

"What's the difference that I came in here? You're already dressed, aren't you?"

"You better watch the way you talk to me. Don't you ever forget that I am your mother."

Stacey looked at the bathtub, and it was more than half full but rapidly draining. Stacey grabbed the plug and stopped the water from emptying.

"Now what the hell are you doing?"

"Showing you how much I regret Dad not taking me with him and leaving me here with you. You are so loving it just makes me feel all warm inside."

Her mother's face reddened. "You can be such a bitch, Stacey!"

"I wonder where I get it from."

"Get out of the bathroom and go to your room. I don't want to see you for the rest of the night. You're a disrespectful and thankless little brat. Look at what I do for you and the way you treat me in return."

"Do you think not being able to see you is some form of punishment? Because if you do I want to tell you it's not. Trust me, I want to see you even less than you want to see me."

Her mother slammed the brush down on the counter, and her eyes were wild with anger. "You're a little bastard like your father, you know that?"

"And you're a bitch that cares about money and men more than her own daughter."

"What did you just say to me?" Her mother marched over to Stacey and swung an open hand wildly, smacking her on the face and shoving her out the door. "You smart ass little kid, you deserve a fist in your mouth.

I suggest you get the hell away from me before I do something I might regret."

Stacey rubbed her cheek. The stinging sensation the slap left behind made her smile. She watched her mother retreat to the mirror and brush her hair as if nothing had happened, muttering profanities under her breath.

"I hate you for what you've done to this family. And I hate you even more for chasing Dad away and then making other men and your work more important than me. You're unloving and cold."

Her mother kicked the door shut with force, but Stacey inserted her foot, stopping it from closing.

"You better remove that foot and get out of my face before I do something to you we're going to both regret."

"Yeah, that's the second time you said that. What are you going to do to me?" Stacey mocked. "Maybe you can smack me again or leave me home alone for days at a time and act like I'm an annoyance when I want to talk to you. You have great parenting skills."

"Get your foot out of the way. Now! I mean it!"

Stacey reached down and grabbed a manageable-sized brick, hit the door with her shoulder, and generated an immense amount of force for someone so small. Her mother stumbled backward and seemed stunned. Stacey charged into the room, lifted the brick over her head, and crashed it on top of her mother's head. Blood spurted and ran down her mother's face as she staggered around, disoriented, and worked desperately to find her balance.

Dropping the brick, Stacey watched her mother struggle to regain her composure for a moment before she charged her and pushed her around the bathroom with the strength of an angry man. The blow to the head took any fight her mother might have had out of her, and Stacey pulled her to the bathtub by grabbing her clothing. She pushed her in and held her head beneath the water, choking her as she did so.

The water turned crimson red from the head wound.

"Here," Stacey said and removed the dollar bill from her pocket with her free hand. She yanked her mother's head out of the water and she opened her mouth wide to suck in air. Stacey shoved the dollar bill into her mouth and slammed her head back down into the water. "If that's more important to you than me, you can choke on it!"

Stacey held her mother beneath the water, watching as the final air bubbles escaped her lungs. Her mother went limp.

"Let her go," Deb said and placed a hand on Stacey's shoulder.

Stacey let go, and the body was somewhere between floating and sinking, hanging halfway out of the bathtub, and still twitching.

Deb lifted her mother's body and slid it into the tub.

"Come, help me load the bricks into her clothing, and we will fill the tub up the rest of the way when we're done weighing her down," Deb said as if she had rehearsed this moment a hundred times. "She's gonna bloat and want to float, so we're going to use every brick you brought up. Maybe we'll need even more. I want to make sure she stays beneath the water."

Crazy Eyes entered the bathroom carrying a large stack of bricks. Stacey flinched and turned away. "No, not him."

"Forget him," Deb said. "You hear me? Forget you've ever seen him."

"He scares me."

"He's helping you right now," Deb said. "Hush yourself before he decides to let you do the dirty work."

Stacey looked at Deb with vacant eyes.

"That's right. Just forget you've seen him."

Both Deb and Crazy Eyes loaded the bricks into her clothing and filled the tub with more water.

"Don't come in here again," Deb said to Stacey. "She got what was coming to her. We will take care of the rest. Maybe we can say the bathroom has a bad clog in it and we can't use it. I don't know how we're going to handle this one yet. I have to think about this and work out the details."

"OK." Stacey said, distant as the stars.

"Go on, get out of here, and don't worry about a thing. I don't even want you thinking about this either. It's being taken care of."

Stacey exited the bathroom and forgot what she was just doing. She went downstairs and turned on the television. Placing her button-eyed doll in her lap, she stroked the string hair and watched whatever was on.

# 27

# THE TUB

*The past.*

"Leave him alone!" Stacey shouted but was fearful to move against the deranged man.

Crazy Eyes ignored her and carried Larry to the bathroom door and kicked it open, breaking the lock. The smell of something awful filled the hallway, and Stacey turned away, covering her nose and mouth with her hands as she gagged.

"You should've minded your own damn business, kid," Crazy Eyes said, and the sound of splashing water drew Stacey's attention.

"Don't look in there," Deb said and tried to turn Stacey away.

"Keep your hands off of me, and stop telling me what to do!" Stacey shouted and shoved Deb.

Deb staggered backward, her eyes wide with disbelief that her sister would thwart her so aggressively.

"You just pushed me!" Deb said. "You dare do that after all I've done for you?"

"You're always telling me what to do," Stacey said, caught somewhere in the middle of dealing with her sister and trying to help Larry. His head was being pushed into the bathtub filled with water and held down. His legs kicked wildly, and Crazy Eyes laughed maniacally. Water splashed everywhere, flooding the floor and soaking the walls.

"Why would you do that to me knowing that whenever I did anything it was to look out for and protect you?" Deb said. Her fists were clenched, and she marched toward Stacey. "I did it to protect us."

"You've been lying to me," Stacey said. "You've lied about who you are and who Crazy Eyes is! You've been lying about who I really am. Playing some sort of game."

"Anything I've ever done was to try and protect you! And so what if it required a little white lie here and there? It has kept you safe, hasn't it?"

Deb grabbed Stacey by the hair and pulled her into the bathroom. "I was trying to save you from having to see this, but now I think you should know what you did and watch your boyfriend pay the price for it."

Stacey was helpless in her sister's clutch. Her hair was tangled around her hand and wrist and she couldn't move an inch. Deb's other hand cupped her chin and kept her eyes forward.

"No," Stacey said. What she saw made her clamp her eyes shut.

"You shoulda stayed across the street and minded your own damn business, kid," Crazy Eyes said. "You punk kids are always making trouble. Making me do things like this."

Larry was slipping on the wet floor, and his fight was becoming less and less. Stacey watched, and as the water calmed with Larry's waning fight, she noticed something that made her pull against her sister's hold. There was ice in the bathwater, and below the surface was a bloated body, possibly weighed down by something. Pruned and white, missing pieces of flesh that floated in the murky water like seaweed, it was difficult to look at and understand.

"What the hell did you do to Mom?" Stacey screamed and thrashed. She threw an elbow and hit Deb on the chin and knocked her down. Deb fell with a heavy thud, releasing her hold. Stacey charged Crazy Eyes and slammed into him. He backpedaled to the wall and crashed into it, losing his footing on the wet floor. Larry lifted his head out of the water and choked and gasped for air.

"Go," Stacey shouted. "Get out while you can!"

Larry skidded across the floor but managed to get his footing. Choking and puking tainted water, he continued to gasp for air as he skipped over Deb's lunging hand. Down the stairs and out the door he went, slamming the door behind him."

"What have you done? You let him get away!" Deb shouted.

"He was innocent," Stacey said. She knelt on the wet floor and looked into the tub.

"Why would you do that after all we've been through together?"

"Because something's not right here. Mom is dead in the bathtub, and you've been trying to preserve her body with ice. You pretended she was on the phone while you brushed me off, and she was here the entire time, disintegrating in the water. You washed her down the drain a little at a time and refilled the tub. That's what you've been doing."

"I did it to protect you!"

"You did this to protect me?" She shook her head in disbelief. "You're harboring a killer, and he just tried drowning our neighbor!"

"Because Larry knew too much, and you allowed him to get too close."

"I hope Larry calls the police," Stacey said. "I've grown tired of you and your telling me what to do. I've grown tired of the lies and living in fear. And Crazy Eyes . . . I don't know why you hang around him."

Larry will go to the police, and they will come and they will arrest you. They will lock you up forever."

"Let them come," Stacey said. "They'll take us all away."

"She doesn't get it," Deb said.

Crazy Eyes stepped forward. "They'll know you killed your mother."

"I didn't kill my mother," Stacey said. "One of you did it."

"No, you killed her because you resented her. She left you home alone and worked a lot to support us and that bothered you."

"I missed her, but I wasn't angry enough to kill her."

Crazy Eyes reached into the bathwater, turning the body and sticking his hand into the mouth of the waterlogged head. He withdrew a dollar bill. "You don't remember telling her how if this was more important to her than you that she could choke on it?"

Stacey sat cross-legged. She closed her eyes and tried not to hear her sister or the man with the crazy eyes anymore. But she did hear them. She heard them scheming and plotting, but she didn't care. Because that's all it seemed Deb ever did. There was something wrong with her.

# 28

# I NEED TO GET OUT

*Present day.*

The sound of blood pumping through her veins. The pulsing beat of her heart. The churning inside her own stomach sounded like a freight train, and yet the silence that infiltrated her ears tore at her psyche and created an unimaginable horror.

The deafening quiet was nothing like she anticipated. She expected it to be soothing and a triumph over the things that haunted her every day and night. The voices. But what she experienced right now was maddening, pushing her over a ledge she stared down every day. And what she remembered about herself nudged her that much closer. She was the embodiment of evil. The monster in the closet. The thing in someone's nightmare.

But mostly she was one that was many. Three at least.

Slats on the walls played tricks on her eyes, and the net floor looked as if it were a snare ready to spring. The chair that had been supplied was as hard as stone, unmovable, and impossible to find comfort on. Her bones creaked in protest as she shifted every few seconds to try to find a comfortable position that just didn't exist.

*Just quit.*

"No," she argued silently with herself. "I need this. I need to find peace. A reprieve from who I am, from what I've done and seen. But mostly I need to forget what they do to me at that place."

*I know who you are.*

The voice in her head was booming, like someone yelling. She cringed at the silent thought that echoed inside like a scream. She struggled through every second, hearing the functions of her own body growing louder, her mind racing faster and faster. Everything going on shouldn't be like this, but yet it was so distracting it took away from her outer physical discomfort and brought it all within, near that unfamiliar voice that was in her. She always thought of it as her quiet side, without the voices and the overstuffed pocket of secrets.

But while she was deep inside the recesses of her mind she saw something dark. It had no feeling, and she knew it completely. It wasn't alone, and it wasn't happy she was here, in this room, and it longed to escape this place and go on a rampage.

*Damn people deserve their suffering.*

*They won't leave us alone.*

She knew that seeing more blood would never quiet the voices. It hadn't before. Just like all those years ago, her actions did nothing to contain them. Most of what she did had been forgotten until now; it reappeared through vivid hallucinations brought on by being locked inside this solitary room of perfect quiet—perfect, disturbing quiet.

In a way she missed what the three of them did together and longed for it more than hunger for a meal. There was nothing like seeing the look in someone's eyes as you strangled them. That's what she did to the girl she tied with the jump rope with the plastic pink handles. The eyes watered, bulged, and fluttered a bit as they slowly dimmed and departed with a soft final exhale.

At least that girl was at peace. Look at how Stacey had had to live. Caged like an animal with unexplainable things running around inside her head trying to cause chaos.

But no matter how hard she tried she couldn't concentrate on these thoughts because they were interfered with by the silence of the room, the sound of the functions of her body, and it was driving her crazy. She needed to know what was at the core, the thing beyond the voices, anger, and aggression, and the secret pocket. That's why she came here, but it was a waste of her time because no matter how hard she tried to get to it, they would just block her. They had more control than she did.

She stood, shaking, no longer able to ignore the fact that she needed to get out and that she'd unearthed too much about herself that should have stayed forgotten. She wanted to belt out a primal scream from frustration but began to pant instead. There were no words. But the thoughts kept coming.

Beast.

Monster.

Killer.

Murderer.

Hurrying to the panic button next to the door, she pushed it and fell to her knees. Everything she'd just experienced was too much to handle all at once. She needed to see the doctor. Not the doctor here, but the one where she came from. Now regretting having left, she wanted to go back. The screams that came from inside her own mind and the ones from other patients were so much better than this, and in so many ways. It was a distraction and had become a way of life for her.

The door opened and Stacey crawled out, panting, sweating, and grunting. She collapsed to the floor, and Doctor Dubreuil hovered over her.

"Margaret, are you all right?" he said and felt her pulse. Ooze ran out of the corner of her mouth. Her eyes were distant dots, and he took off his lab coat and covered her with it. She was shivering.

Running to a box mounted on the wall, he yanked it open and pulled out a red telephone. "I think the reporter might be seizing," he said in a hurry. "Send someone in and call an ambulance immediately!"

With unseen force, the doctor was slammed into the wall hard, his head glancing off the mounted box, the phone falling out of his hand. A gash on the side of his head opened up and bled badly.

Stacey picked up the phone and handed it to the doctor.

"She's attacking me," he shouted. "Please call the police!"

She ripped the phone from his hand, hit him in the head with it, and slammed it down. With one hand she dragged the stunned doctor into the room she'd just come out of. Extremely strong for a girl of her stature, she didn't struggle at all to move the average-sized man. A small trail of blood followed them into the room.

"What are you doing?" he said.

Stacey retrieved his jacket and put it on. She took notice of the pens in the breast pocket, removed one, and held it like a knife.

"Uhh," she grunted, showing him her weapon and motioning at the room with her chin. She looked around, curious in every way.

"It's an anechoic chamber," the doctor said. "You volunteered to come in here to do a news report for your work. You are safe now. I don't know if you're still hallucinating or what's happening."

Stacey took her time and finished buttoning up the smock one hole at a time and brushed it smooth with both hands. She looked at the doctor and saw a ring of keys on his belt.

"God damn," the doctor said and rubbed his head, checking the blood on his hand. "You hit me really hard, and I'm feeling really dizzy. I think you might have given me a concussion."

She pointed at the keys, held out a hand, and wiggled her fingers. "Uh."

He fumbled with the keys at first, his hands shaking, but he managed to unclip them, and he handed them to her.

"Uh," she said and pointed at the door.

The doctor showed her the key she was looking for. Stacey stepped out of the room, locked the door, and turned out the light. She heard the doctor screaming, and although his voice was muted, she could feel his fear as she pressed her back against the wall and slid down into a sitting position. It was a good distraction, his fear and screams. They reminded her of her room, and she would relish in it while she was able.

She dropped the keys, looked at her hands and feet, and reflected. The sounds of the things that moved within her own body distracted her just enough to keep her away from the thing inside her core where she believed the others didn't dwell. She almost got to the thing that was her—or that could have been her without the others. But she couldn't take what she was experiencing and had to get out.

At least she couldn't hear the sound of the blood moving through her body any longer. There was something greater than her own thoughts and her constant confusion, and for right now she was OK with it because she had gotten within arm's reach of peace.

"Put your hands where I can see them," a police officer said and had a Taser centered at her chest, the red dot swinging around menacingly.

Stacey looked at her feet, unafraid of the weapon, and went back to studying her hands. Did she even control these things or did the other things inside her do that? Her hair dangled toward her feet and created a false veil where she could hide while she pondered that question.

"I said to put your hands where I can see them!"

That voice meant nothing to her. The things she would hear at night, during the day, and even now, the people who had blamed her for their deaths were so much more commandeering. It was never-ending and maddening and allowed her no chance to forget or to care about anything. But as cruel as that room was, she did forget for just a fleeting moment. It was when she quit and crawled out of the room. And that moment was better than her getting near that inner peace she was seeking because she was able to forget about the voices. She escaped them, and that meant there was a way she could silence them. Uncertain how to replicate that, she rested her head back with a smile. There was a way to escape them. Maybe there was a victory in this after all.

"Lower your weapon, Sergeant," someone commanded, and the sergeant holstered his weapon as instructed.

A doctor was being escorted into the hallway by another police officer. The doctor who was locked in the room banged on the inside door, begging to be let out.

"Someone let him out," Doctor Lee said. "Stacey!" She hurried to her side and knelt.

Stacey looked over Doctor Lee's shoulder with a gaze that was distant.

"Please, back away and give me some room," Doctor Lee said. "This woman is a patient of mine. She escaped from Sunnyside Capable Care Mental Institution earlier today and has been under my supervision for years."

The doctor came out of the chamber and pointed at Stacey. "She hit me in the head with a phone and threatened to stab me with a pen!"

"She's not under your care anymore, Doctor," the sergeant said to Doctor Lee. "She assaulted someone and will be taken into custody. Charges will be filed, and a judge will set bail tomorrow."

"No," the other officer said, obviously of higher rank. "We've been looking for her, and we're glad we found her before she really hurt someone."

"Besides," Doctor Lee said. "You don't have the resources to care for her. Are you educated in mental illness and multiple personality disorders?"

"No."

"This woman is withdrawn and cannot follow simple instructions. She is in her own world, and whatever is going on inside her mind is what dictates her actions. We must get her back to her room where her surroundings are familiar. Then I'll begin to regulate her with proper medications and sessions of conversation."

Doctor Lee helped Stacey to her feet. "You've grown up to be such a pretty young lady, and I've enjoyed our friendship," she said to Stacey. "Why did you leave? I was so upset to find you had wandered off without telling me."

Although unresponsive, Stacey seemed to take to the sound of Doctor Lee's voice.

"Come, let's get you out of this silly smock and get you home. Maybe we can talk there. I would love to hear what happened."

# 29

# CARNAGE

*The past.*

A stampede of heavy footsteps climbing the wooden stairs behind Stacey meant nothing. The carnage before her was a display of the grizzly nature of people—which included herself. After all, she might not have killed her mother, but she killed the boy on that path with the rock. And her stepfather.

A large man stepped past her, his weapon drawn. "Are you hurt?"

She didn't hear him. She only saw her mother's bloated, decaying body weighed down in the bathtub filled with murky water and ice, suspended in a state of nothingness. She tried to imagine what it would be like to be in there with her but couldn't because all of the nothingness around her came slamming into her head, and she was suddenly fearful.

She spider-crawled backward and slammed into the wall, her eyes wide with inexplicable terror. She tried to understand why all these people were invading her home. Their guns were drawn, and their uniforms and badges meant something of authority. She was just a young girl, left all alone in the middle of this massacre. Left to take the blame for all of it.

What if they found out she killed that boy on the path?

She had to deny it like Deb said so they wouldn't know.

What if they asked her about her stepdad?

She would have to stick to the story Deb told her.

"Are you hurt?" the officer said again, holstering his weapon.

Stacey looked at him. Middle-aged and kind-faced, he seemed to genuinely care about her well-being. She blinked hard, knowing care was overrated.

"Is the ambulance here yet?" he said, pivoting on the balls of his feet. "And someone get me a blanket or something."

"The ambulance is about a minute out," someone said.

Stacey noticed a tremble in her body slamming her teeth together and shaking her limbs. There was something terribly wrong with her on the inside. Lost and confused, she had been beaten down by someone who was supposed to love her and had promised to protect her. Deb had broken her heart. Destroyed her trust.

"Just when you think you've seen it all," the officer said and wrapped her with a blanket. He carried her out of the room and down the flight of stairs. "Who is home with you?"

"My sister and this guy with really weird eyes," Stacey said.

"Are they still here? We checked the entire house, and you're the only one we found. Who is that in the bathtub, do you know?"

"They killed her," Stacey said. She watched her mother over the officer's shoulder until she couldn't see her anymore.

"Who killed her?"

"My sister and the guy with the crazy eyes."

The officer placed her down on a stretcher with a soft mattress and cuffed her wrist. He used the other side of the cuff to secure her to the raised rail.

Looking left, Stacey could see Larry standing on the sidewalk with his parents, wrapped lovingly in their embrace. She didn't want to see that so she looked away. Love was something she didn't know how to handle—no matter how hard she tried to pretend to know. Surveying the front of her house, she saw Deb and Crazy Eyes standing in a window upstairs looking down on her. They were talking to each other, plotting their next move, but they quickly moved out of sight.

Stacey wondered: How can't they see them?

# 30

# THE NEXT DAY

*Present day.*

Doctor Lee stood outside Stacey's door inside Sunnyside Capable Care. Director Conroy looked into the small window with Doctor Lee.

"Any ideas as to why she went there?" Conroy said.

"Plenty of ideas, but one theory."

"And?"

"I think she went there to escape whatever it is that haunts her here. She was seeking silence, hoping to drown out the voices. I think she was trying to discover her true self."

Director Conroy rubbed his chin, fiddled with his glasses, and groaned deep in his throat as if the revelation had never occurred to him. "Isn't that room silent enough? She doesn't even talk."

"It was a highly intelligent move if you ask me," Doctor Lee said. "In my assessment, the conflict insider her mind is never-ending."

"How could she know about that place?"

Doctor Lee pulled a magazine out of her briefcase and opened it to a marked page. "She's been reading."

"Reading?"

"I figured if she wasn't going to talk, I'd try reading with her. A magazine and an article was enough to inspire her. Like I said, it was a highly intelligent move."

"Huh," Conroy said and paused. "What are the chances that she walks into that place only to have the woman who was scheduled to take part in the experiment to have been in a fatal auto accident less than an hour before?"

Doctor Lee looked over her shoulder. "It seems Death has a sense of humor."

"Well I'm not laughing."

"No, none of us are."

Doctor Lee neatened her smock and knocked on the door. "Excuse me, Director, I'd like to see if Stacey is in the talking mood."

Director Conroy spun on his heel and walked down the long hallway. "It seems you're the one with the sense of humor today, Doctor Lee."

"Director?"

He looked over his shoulder.

"I'd really like to know how Stacey was able to just up and walk away from the group while they were tending to the garden. I find that troublesome."

"I'm already working on that." He faded down the hallway muttering, "Believe me I'm already working on that."

Doctor Lee entered the room and closed the door. She watched Stacey for a moment, hating the silence this poor girl had to endure. She'd come into the asylum as a child and had now grown into a young woman. She would live out the rest of her life within these walls, and that was a sad fact.

Stacey had been sitting on the bed cross-legged, and she was looking out the barred window, her stare distant and untouched.

"How are you feeling today?" Doctor Lee said.

Stacey continued to stare, undisturbed.

"I thought you were going to speak to me yesterday, you know that?"

Still there was silence.

"You know if you have something you'd like to tell me, I'd really like to hear it. Maybe there's something you'd like to tell me about what you saw or might have learned about yourself while you were in that room?"

Stacey stared some more, and Doctor Lee tried to see what she was looking at.

"Are you looking at the plants that were put in yesterday?"

A garden of annuals mixed with bright oranges, reds, yellows, and purples were bursting with color.

"They're gorgeous, I know. You were supposed to help put them in, but you walked away. Do you want to tell me how you did that without anyone noticing?"

Stacey remained still.

"Or how you knew how to navigate around in public when you haven't been outside these walls in over ten years? What were you looking for?"

Still, Stacey was quiet and unmoved.

"I had a patient some years back who would focus on one flower outside his window. You remind me of him in so many ways, and like him, I wish you'd acknowledge me . . . let me know you can hear me and tell me what troubles you. Maybe I can help."

Stacey was like a statue.

"Please tell me, Stacey. I know I can help you."

Doctor Lee set the magazine down in front of her, turned to the page that explained about the anechoic chamber. Tears welled up in her patient's eyes.

"Oh, Stacey, I'm so sorry," Doctor Lee said, and wished Stacey's tears were a sign that she was being heard. But Doctor Lee knew it most likely meant nothing at all. She'd seen Stacey cry before . . . a prisoner in her own body and inside this room.

"Do you remember leaving Sunnyside yesterday and walking all the way to a lab?"

Stacey exhaled.

"You know about that room because you read the article about it. You went there on purpose. That means you are in there, paying attention. Why won't you break your silence and talk to me?"

Stacey looked at Doctor Lee and motioned to speak, her mouth opening and rounding out. But her mouth closed as if she were taking in a lungful of silence, and she looked out the window again. Her eyes were glassy, as if something inside was trying to communicate but couldn't, and she was showing the signs of frustration.

Doctor Lee moved close to her, placed a hand on her back, and rubbed it. "I know it's hard for you. I'm here for you. I want you to remember that. When you're ready to talk about it, I'll be here and ready to listen to whatever it is you have to say. You should try and get some rest."

Doctor Lee got up and left the magazine behind. She exited the room.

# 31

# VOICES

*Present day.*

"Now that you remember everything," a voice said from a darkened corner, "does it make you feel any better?"

Stacey shook her head.

"You were so young, and still you got so many. Your silence means nothing to them. They know underneath that vow of silence there is a monster, and they're going to keep you stupid with medicine and make you grow old in here."

Stacey tried to ignore what Deb was saying to her and concentrated on the sound of the door closing as Dr. Lee departed.

"I can't stand listening to that doctor talking. She's annoying and maybe someday soon you can get her and shut her up for good."

"Uh," Stacey mumbled and shook her head.

"You say that now, and that's OK. We've got all the time in the world to help you change your mind," Deb said. "She's not your friend. We are."

"The little girl you lured out of the house with the jump rope and choked to death," Crazy Eyes said. Stacey looked around. She didn't know where he was yet. He usually hid in the shadows. "And the boy you smashed in the face with a jagged rock." A laugh. "Don't you remember the surge of adrenaline that gave you as you looked at the life leaving his fractured body?"

Stacey lowered her head, trying desperately not to listen to them, not to remember. But their voices sounded like they were coming from inside her own head sometimes. Deep down where the pocket of secrets was kept. Maybe they were the ones protecting those secrets and trying to keep them hidden.

"And our stepfather? You pushed him down the stairs for no good reason other than you wanted to," Deb said. "How does that make you feel?"

"Just like when you drowned your own mother. Hating her for trying to provide for you after you took your stepfather's life. She tried to protect you because she knew what you did. She said he fell. And how did you pay her back? By attacking her and submerging her in cold bathwater, dumping ice on the body every day to try and keep her from stinking. You can put my face on all you'd like. It doesn't change who and what you are."

Stacey slapped her hands over her ears.

"Draining the bathwater to wash away the flesh that began to separate from her body and refilling the tub day after day."

"You're very cunning at a very young age."

"But we were the ones always cleaning up after you."

Stacey began to rock back and forth.

"But what about the two that got away?"

Stacey stopped rocking and looked around the room.

"Do you think about them and how it might have been if we had finished the job?"

Stacey shook her head.

"Larry, the one responsible for turning you in and getting you put here. I told you boys are trouble, and you didn't listen to me."

Stacey looked around the room. Nothing changed about the painted white concrete walls. Maybe it wasn't that bad in here. If only they would shut up.

"And what about that boy, Beau? The one you tried to kill by pushing him off of the playground?"

She liked him and was sorry for what she'd done but couldn't say so and didn't want to think it. It was as if they could hear her every thought. She liked them both, and Doctor Lee, too. She was good company and kept Deb and Crazy Eyes quiet whenever she was around. But they wouldn't allow Stacey to talk, and Doctor Lee would tire and leave only to have Deb and Crazy Eyes come out again. It was a vicious cycle.

Crazy Eyes stepped out of the corner, and Deb did, too, each coming from the opposite side of the room. They sat on the bed next to her. Deb clung to the magazine and swung her legs. Crazy Eyes just stared at her.

Stacey lowered her head and hid behind the curtain of hair again, closing her eyes and trying desperately not to listen to what they were saying. But she knew she would have to hear them because they were a part of her. The part that made up her pocket of secrets but split three ways. And whichever one came out and used her body was dependent upon the situation she was in.

She hated all three of them equally and should've found that bridge or tall building instead of that room. She lost herself in the thought of trying to fly.

# EPILOGUE

# A GUIDING HAND

*Present day.*

Margaret ached badly. Suspended upside down, blood dripped. The seat belt held her firmly in place. Disoriented, she looked around. Trees, a fast-moving stream swollen with rainwater, the continued pitter-patter of the rainfall, and the strong smell of smoke and oil filled her senses.

She tried to move, to free herself, but she couldn't. The seat belt was locked and tight. Her head hurt, and her vision went in and out of focus. She shook her head to try to fight the feeling, but a blackness overcame her and threatened to pull her under.

"Margaret," the voice of a woman said.

Pulled from the black, she focused on a big woman with short hair.

"We're going to help you get out of there. Stay calm," she said.

Margaret wanted to reply but felt strange.

"Tammy, honey, I'm going to need you to crawl in there and unclip that seat belt," the woman said. "Go in through the other side of the car."

Margaret watched in disbelief as a child climbed into the wreckage with her. The kid found the seat belt clip but struggled with it.

"You'll be OK, miss. Mara will help you through this," Tammy said. "She's a good person and always helps those in need. She doesn't have much patience for those that are bad though."

Tammy pressed the button, and with a click the seat belt let Margaret go, dropping her onto the ceiling inside the vehicle. Before she could

153

get her bearings, two strong hands grabbed her underneath the armpits, dragged her out of the wreckage, and stood her up.

"How do you feel?" Mara said.

"A little shaken up, I guess," Margaret said. Her pain was gone. "The little girl that went in there to get me out?" She turned to look.

"Hey now," Mara said. "There's no reason for you to look at that car. There's nothing good there." Mara held Margaret's arm and kept her from looking at the wreckage. "Tammy's coming out now."

"Thank you," Margaret said and looked up the steep embankment and wondered how anyone could survive that. She saw a massive crowd gathered atop the hill, and she waved at them. "I'm OK."

No one responded, and she found that odd.

"They can't hear you," Mara said and brushed debris off of Tammy.

"Oh," Margaret said. She cupped her hands around her mouth and shouted, "I'm down here, and I'm OK."

Still, no one atop the hill responded. They looked down at the gorge in horror.

"No matter how loud you yell, they won't be able to hear you," Mara said.

Margaret looked at Mara and the children with her. These last few moments were odd.

"Come with me," Mara said. "Let's get the children to safety, and I'll get someone to help you."

Margaret hesitated, looking up the hillside.

"Come," Mara said and gave her arm a gentle tug. "Don't think too much about it. This will all make sense in a little while. For now, I need your help in bringing the children to safety. Will you concentrate your energy there and help me with that?"

Margaret nodded. "Yes, I can do that." She followed the small group upstream, leaving her overturned car and physical body behind.

"Thank you," Mara said. "I'm sorry you were chosen to be a part of a plan to give someone else a chance at working at finding themself. He must have plans for her that I cannot comprehend. I know there was much more you wanted to accomplish yourself. But Sariel knows what he's doing, and as much as it is a mystery to me, there are plans that are sometimes greater than ourselves."

"Who is Sariel?"

"You'll meet him soon enough," Mara said. "For now, let's help these children."

# BOOKS BY
# KEITH ROMMEL

**Shade of the Reaper Series**
*The Cursed Man*
*The Lurking Man*
*The Sinful Man*
*The Silent Woman*

**Devil Tree Series**
*The Devil Tree*
*The Devil Tree II*

*The White River Monster*
*Ice Canyon Monster*